MW0037734q

The
Ambidextrist

Also by Peter Rock

This Is the Place
Carnival Wolves

Peter
Rock

Context Books

The
Ambidextrist

to DAVID AND EUGENIA
LOVELY PEOPLE
MY FRIENDS,
PETER ROCK
your toastmaster

New York 2002

www.contextbooks.com

Designer: Johanna Roebas
Jacket design: Archie Ferguson

Context Books
368 Broadway
Suite 314
New York, NY 10013

Library of Congress Cataloging-in-Publication Data

Rock, Peter, 1967-
    The ambidextrist : a novel / Peter Rock.
      p. cm.
    ISBN 1-893956-22-9 (hardcover)
1. Drifters—Fiction. 2. Homeless persons—Fiction. 3. Philadelphia
(Pa.)—Fiction. 4. Schuylkill River Valley (Pa.)—Fiction.   I. Title.
  PS3568.O327 A8 2002
  813'.54—dc21
                                                    2001005303
ISBN 1-893956-22-9

9 8 7 6 5 4 3 2 1

Manufactured in the United States of America

For Ella

It has been raining for three days.
The faces of the giants
on the billboards
still smile.

—Charles Reznikoff

One

First Crossing

The four boys snatch the tattered magazine from each other, cursing when it rips and then trying to pull single pages free. It's late. They stand beneath an overpass, light filtering down, the silent black river on one side and the empty train tracks on the other. The boys are nervous, excited; they are only thirteen.

"Man," Terrell says. "These ladies are licking each other."

"You haven't seen anything." Darnay laughs. He kicks at the small pile of things they've found, hidden under some old boards, inside a plastic bag. Taking out a pair of pants, he pulls them on over his shorts, as a joke. He cinches the leather belt around his waist.

Down river, lighted letters circle atop the Peco Building: PHILADELPHIA BELIEVES. A truck rattles past, overhead. Headlights shine, glancing across the water, and disappear.

"Let's get out of here," John says.

"Scared?" Swan says. He spills jars from the bag, along the ground. "Baby food," he says. "No money."

And then, beyond the train tracks, the bushes begin to shake and rustle. First to one side, then the other, as if a number of people are about to emerge. A scream rises, and a dark shape suddenly breaks loose, lunging closer, shouting sounds that aren't quite words.

The boys turn and run, stumbling on the rough gravel, downriver, pages of the magazine still in their hands. Their backs crawl, bowed out, ready to be touched.

"Wait," John says, lagging behind. "No one's following."

They slow and look behind them, not stopping until they're certain.

One man stands there, fifty yards away, illuminated by the faint light of the Vine Street on-ramp. If he's still screaming, they can't hear him. His body reflects slightly, his shoulders padded or hunched somehow. He kicks his legs out, his feet pointed; his arms are above his head, and he keeps twisting and kicking, all in slow motion.

"White guy," John says.

"There's just him," Darnay says, embarrassed for running. "We could go back."

"Not now," Terrell says. "He might have friends."

2

═ Two
═ Questions

The next morning, Scott still wears his greenish-blue jacket. Some smooth cross between leather and vinyl, it looks like it belongs to a marching-band uniform, with finger-sized wooden buttons that fit through loops, all down the front, and epaulets of dirty gold twine resting on his thin shoulders. His jeans are tight, faded at the knees, seams split a few inches to make room for his cowboy boots. His hair, combed but not quite clean, hangs almost to his collar; his face, shaved smooth, is thin and pale, his squinting eyes set close together. He smiles at Lisa Roberts, relentlessly, and his teeth shine so white and even, so at odds with the rest of him, that they do not seem real.

"Thirty years old," Lisa says, shuffling through papers. "One hundred and thirty pounds. Has there been any fluctuation in your weight?"

They are sitting in her narrow office, their knees inches apart, her desk taking up half the room. Scott slides the soles of his boots along the carpet, sharp toes pointing right at her, then pulls the boots back

3

before they touch her foot. He folds his left leg over his right one. Lisa is not a doctor, yet she wears a white coat with her name embroidered in red above the pocket. He feels her eyes on him, looking him over, sizing him up. A magnetic paper-clip holder stands on her desk, surrounded by all the dried-up pens she set aside before finding the one she uses now to write on a clipboard. In the window behind her, a tiny airplane, hardly moving, climbs into the sky.

"Has your weight been steady?" she says.

"I know what fluctuation means," Scott says. "And no, no fluctuation, none that I know of. Not that I spend a lot of time weighing myself." As he speaks, he gestures with his hands; blue-and-pink feathers swing from a roach clip attached to his jacket collar.

"You say you've been in Philadelphia three months," Lisa says. "What brought you here?"

Scott can tell by how she is sitting, how she leans away, that she is uneasy, that she wishes she was the one closest to the door.

"You have family here?" she says. "Planned to meet someone?"

"I heard it's a serious city," he says, "so I wanted to try it out. I mean, there might be bigger ones—hell, there are bigger ones—but there aren't any that are more serious." He looks up at the acoustic-tile ceiling, the fluorescent light flickering at him. That answer is the truth, partly; it is also true that he plans to meet someone, a woman, though he does not yet know who she is.

Out the window, the city spreads itself. The office they sit in is on the ninth floor of the university hospital, and he can see buildings, full of people, people driving in cars and walking in the streets below, disappearing under trees. Wires and signs fill the air.

"And your last employer was Kenny Rogers?" Lisa Roberts says.

"That's true, technically. I been all over, since then."

"Have you ever been convicted of a criminal offense?"

"No, I have not. Did you want to hear more about Kenny?"

"We have a lot of questions, here," Lisa Roberts says.

"Shoot, then."

"Do you believe you get enough exercise?"

"I stay in shape," he says. "Jujitsu. That's a martial art."

"Yes," she says. "What would you say is your best characteristic?"

"Perspicacity," he says. "That means being real clear-sighted, if you didn't know. Real acute."

"And what would you say is your greatest weakness?"

"I'm pretty gullible," he says. "I can really get taken in."

That is a lie, but he's found it works sometimes, opens people up a little. He wonders if perhaps being gullible is the opposite of perspicacity, and if that is what Lisa Roberts is writing now. He tries to read her face for some reaction, for some indication—they always say there are no right or wrong answers, but that isn't true. Looking at her, he bets she is ten years older than he is, that she takes a shower every day. She wears dark tights, without any runs that he can see; perhaps her toes poke through inside her shoes, or the skin of her heel shows. A framed picture of a man with thick sideburns rests on the back of her desk, and other frames hold two little girls, on either side. The same girl, Scott decides, at different ages.

"Gullible," Lisa says, writing it down. "Have you ever taken medication for depression?"

"No."

"Ever considered suicide?"

"Never."

"Do you feel others are better, smarter, and better-looking than you?"

"I reckon they're out there," he says, "but I try not to think about them too much."

"Are you satisfied with your current state of sexual activity?"

"Just how personal is this going to get?" Scott says. He is not answered, and he pauses, trying to figure how to slow the questions, so he can get some purchase on the situation.

"No," he says softly. "I'm not. Now what would you say is your best characteristic?"

5

"Sorry," Lisa Roberts says. "We don't have time for that. I ask the questions, you answer them."

"Feel a little rude, just talking about myself the whole time."

"Well, this isn't exactly a social conversation."

He shrugs, as if to say he knew that. He wants to tell her not to underestimate, not to disrespect him, but she's already resumed her questioning.

"Does it often seem," she says, "that objects or shadows are really people or animals, or that noises are actually peoples' voices?"

"No," he says.

"When you look at a person, or at yourself in the mirror, have you ever seen the face change right before your eyes?"

Scott leans close, his eyes on her, then eases himself back again.

"Are you the same person who asked me that last question?" he says.

"Yes," she says, and begins writing.

"Easy there," he says. "I was only joking with you—I never see anything like that."

"Seriousness is necessary," Lisa Roberts says. "We need to be certain of a few things, so when we administer the tests to you we can compare the results to those of our schizophrenic patients. You're part of what we call the 'normal control group.'"

"Not yet, I'm not," he says. "First I got to answer the questions, and you still got to check my piss, my urine, and all that."

"Right," she says.

"That'll be clean." He pulls at the roach clip on his jacket. "You might of noticed this, here—it's just for decoration. Found it somewhere. I'm clean." He almost stands to speak, thinking it might help her believe him. "I'm a perfect specimen—that's why I do this. I mean, not that I turn any money down, but I want you-all to learn something from it."

"Are you nervous?" Lisa says.

Questions

"This is just a real different situation. It's a little disorientating, all these questions."

"That's normal," she says. "Feeling that way."

"Then I'm off on the right foot."

"Take this piece of paper, fold it once, and put it on the floor."

Scott does so, then watches Lisa pick it up.

"I heard they're going to take pictures of my brain," he says. "While I'm thinking. Here's a thing that'll interest you to know—I'm ambidextrous. Right hand, left hand, that's all the same to me. Could help the tests, what with the hemispheres of my brain and everything. It'd be like testing two people for the price of one. Right brain, left brain, all that business."

"Do you play any musical instruments?" she says.

"No," he says. "What would that tell you?"

"Just curious," she says. "Your jacket made me wonder."

"It would be easier," he says, "if I knew which questions are part of the test and which ones aren't."

"Would that cause you to change your answers?"

"No," Scott says, after a pause. "Forget it."

"Now," Lisa says, "how about some true-false questions?"

"True," he says.

"Answer these questions as they apply to you," she says, ignoring his joke. "My body parts, or my skin, sometimes seem strange and not belonging to me."

"False."

"People don't always appreciate me."

"True."

"I see things or people around me that others do not see."

"Maybe the connections between them," he says.

"Pardon me?"

When Scott raises his hand to scratch his ear, the arm of his jacket

7

slides roughly along his side and she wrinkles her nose at the raspy sound. She winces, as if he might strike her.

"False," he says, feeling himself on the verge of a wrong answer.

"I've made some real mistakes in the people I've picked as friends."

The questions keep coming, easier if he does not think too much about the reasons, all the times behind his answers. His only friends are those he's met on the street, or in trials at the drug companies. They are only acquaintances, not friends to trust. The last person he trusted was Chrissie; the two of them hitchhiked all the way to Montana, made plans together. Redheaded, she was going to be his woman forever, he believed, and the two of them would live in a pale blue house, rising in the middle of the night to feed the baby, never tiring of each other. She always surprised him, and he trusted her beyond anything. Now he doesn't even know where she is.

"Sometimes my temper explodes," Lisa says.

"False," Scott says, taking a moment to answer. "I got a real cool head."

"I'm quiet when I first meet strangers."

"True."

"Most people would rather win than lose."

"Obviously true," he says.

"There are people that can read minds."

"There's some good guessers," he says. "People who can see ahead, or they've been there before and they can guess. 'Find out what happens before what happens happens'—that's a motto I heard."

"Is that a 'false'?"

"Yes."

In the pause between questions, he listens to the scratch of Lisa's pen, marking the boxes with his answers. Squinting, he can see the colors of the billboards through the window, too distant to read. They cast rectangular shadows onto the highway; what must be cars disappear into the shadows, then emerge out the other side. Clouds cast their

8

own shadows over buildings, white reflections sliding across windows as the office towers rise, tall across the river. Looking at them, he wonders where he'll sleep tonight. This morning, like the morning before, he awoke in an office building that is under construction; he descended two floors, to where the water is hooked up, and as he passed down the hall he suddenly realized that there were men through the open doorways. The men sat at desks, writing with pens, talking on phones, in rooms that had been empty only yesterday. Tonight, he'll have to find a new place.

Since arriving in Philadelphia, he has slept in a vacant lot, behind an old couch with dirty stuffed animals perched in a line, staring out, some missing their plastic eyes; he has slept under an overpass, felt the vibrations of big trucks as they passed a foot above his head. He has spent nights on steam grates, next to men with icicles in their beards from all the frozen condensation—in the morning, he pulled down his pants and the grid showed on his skin, his bare ass scored like a piece of chicken.

"I think that about does it," Lisa Roberts says. "I'm sure we'll be in touch, probably sometime next week. All this information—the phone and address—is correct?"

"Right," he says. "Only the phone's not working. I can just drop by here, at the hospital."

"You'd be paid every two weeks."

"Whatever," he says. "Maybe what you learn from me can help some people. The money's no big deal."

"That's what they all say."

Scott does not stand. He is ready to answer more questions—he wouldn't mind answering them all day and night. It has been a long time since anyone paid him so much attention, took such an interest. He speaks as Lisa ruffles through the papers, putting them in order.

"I watched you when I came in," he says. "Sizing me up—my hair and my coat and everything. What else do you want to know?"

"We're done," she says.

"Anything at all."

"Next they'll do the blood tests."

"One more question," he says. "I know you have one. You're curious about me."

"All right," she says, snapping the metal jaw of the clipboard on the papers it holds. "Tell me this: Do you always smile like that?"

"Try to," he says. "You probably want to know why."

"If it's short."

"Explanation's real simple—it goes back to horses, and that's a thing where I've had some experience. It's so easy to spook a horse. It's because of the shape of their eyes; they can be looking back, watching you while you're riding, at the same time as they look around at where they're going." Scott holds a finger up at each side of his head, pointing in front of, then behind him. "If you're smiling, that makes them relax and behave, since they think you're a happy and kind person."

"There are no horses here," Lisa Roberts says. Her clipboard is on the desk, the cap on her pen. She stands and opens the door.

— Three
— Snake

B ehind the art museum, Scott finds a path that switches back and forth down the slope to the Schuylkill River. Overgrown grass, tangled with shreds of plastic and other trash, stretches out at the bottom, under a few trees and around a dry fountain; green-roofed buildings, their windows boarded up, stand to one side. The air smells of sulfur. He keeps moving, all the way to the railing. The river slides darkly by, forty feet below, a walkway right at its edge. A man sits on the walkway, only his legs visible, stretched out, his feet dangling over the water.

"Hey!" Scott says, then repeats himself, more loudly. "Hey!"

There's a spiral staircase to his left, and he descends, his boots ringing on the metal steps. He hurries along the path.

"And just what is your problem?" the man says.

"What kind of a name is that for a river, anyway?" Scott says. He looks out over the water, its surface almost black, greasy, impossible to see through. "I can't even pronounce it."

"That name's from a whole other language. Means 'hidden river.'" The man doesn't look up to speak. His hair is black, in a short Afro, barely darker than his skin; his beard is pure white. He wears a pink dress shirt and brown slacks. His feet are bare—a pair of rubber sandals rests next to him—and a length of fishing line is tied around one big toe, stretching down into the dark water.

"What's so hidden about it?" Scott says. "It's right there, in plain sight."

"It's thick down there," the man says. "No one knows what all's in the water. Could send scuba divers under and they couldn't tell you a thing."

"You fishing?"

"Just counting the dead fish floating past—they die trying to breathe that water."

"Could get your toe pulled off," Scott says. "Fishing like that."

"This here's just the way Huck Finn did it." The man lifts his foot, wiggles his toes, the nails thick and yellow. "You ever read that book?"

"Of course I read it," Scott says, though he hasn't.

"Name's Ray. Sit down, if you like."

"I'm all right," Scott says. He stands silently, watching Ray whittle at a stick. The knife has a six-inch blade; the stick is taking the shape of a lizard or crocodile. Scott leans closer, wishing he had a knife.

"Where you from?"

"Here," Scott says.

"Wrong," Ray says, snorting back a laugh. "And those boots—couldn't run in those."

"I got no reason to run."

"You will." Ray smiles. He reaches out and slaps the top of Scott's boot. "Know what they say about guys with small feet?"

"No," Scott says, "I sure don't."

"Me neither."

"Thought you were going to trash talk me there," Scott says. "That would have been a mistake."

Snake

Across the river, cars race along the highway, glinting all different colors. Ray lifts his foot and moves it side to side, as if enticing or hypnotizing the fish below.

"What are you working on?" Scott says.

"Nothing in particular," Ray says, but instead of showing it he slides the wood he's been carving into his pocket. His hand, now empty, jerks toward the sky without warning; his leg flexes, as if it might kick. "Just found whittling's a good thing to be doing," he says, "when you're alone in the city. Gives you an excuse to have a knife in your hand, and that reminds people to keep their distance."

"And if they don't?"

"I always hope I don't have to use it." Ray shrugs, still holding the knife. "Down here it's a bunch of crackheads, and you never know what they'll do, how they'll react, who they'll take you for. So you never want to stand too close, never within arm's reach." Waving the knife as he speaks, he pushes Scott back a little, with his free hand.

"I'm clean," Scott says. "And I don't know where it was I started asking for advice."

"I like you," Ray says. "You got a stupid kind of charm. Kind of clueless, kind of reckless, you know what I'm saying?"

"No, I don't." Scott stares out across the river.

"Whether you asked for it and whether you need it," Ray says. "Those two aren't the same thing."

"Whatever," Scott says. He claps his hands, trying to laugh it off, and as he shakes his head, looking down at his feet, all at once he sees the long black shape at the edge of the path. It's pointed right at him.

"Snake!" Shouting, he leaps sideways, almost into the river, and then farther back. At the cry, Ray slides to his feet and dances in the other direction, searching the ground with his eyes, his hands held out flat in front of him.

"Where?" he says. "Where?"

Scott is moving in slow motion now, which seems to have stopped the snake's progress. He points to where it rests—almost two feet long, poised to strike, a shiny, slippery black.

Laughing, Ray leans forward and picks up the snake by the tail. He whips it closer, laughing even harder as Scott stumbles backward.

"How was I to know it's dead?" Scott says.

Ray only smiles. Even barefoot, he is still a head taller than Scott. The fishing line is now wrapped around his ankles; the lead weight and the worm on its hook trail out behind him. Setting the snake back on the ground, he begins untangling himself.

"Snake?" he says. "This is a damn eel. Caught it myself, half an hour ago. Was about to ask if you wanted to share a little with me. Good eating."

"That's not right," Scott says, recovering himself. "I remember what you said before, about the dirt in the water."

"Fish got gills, so they just pass it all through, they filter it out. That's obvious." Ray sits down again, lowering the line after checking his hook. "It's not what's in the water that you got to worry about," he says. "It's what's up on the land."

"I can handle myself on the land," Scott says.

"Seen it all down here," Ray is saying. "Found dead bodies, everything. You want to get yourself into that situation where a person sees you and doesn't see you—where they know you don't have anything they want."

"Are you even talking to me?" Scott says. "I didn't ask for a lecture, and I never believed you were going to eat that eel."

"Those boots," Ray says, shaking his head. He takes out a new pack of Kools, lights one, and shakes one out toward Scott, who doesn't take it.

Ray sets the cigarette down, still burning, and resumes his carving. It is quiet except for the hollow sound of the cars, carried across the river, the rasp as the knife shaves curls from the stick. From time to time, the old man's legs twitch, his arms jerk out straight; he pulls them back under control without a word, then picks up his cigarette and takes another drag.

"All these buildings here with the green roofs," Scott says. "What are those about? That part of Fairmount Park? I seen all the mansions, further up. I know all about that."

"City owns it," Ray says. "Waterworks, used to be, long time ago. Can't sleep in there, if that's what you're thinking."

"I got a place to stay," Scott says.

"They'll get you for trespassing, on top of the vagrancy. After the water got so dirty, they used it for an aquarium, but the seals kept dying. Had a Olympic-type swimming pool on the other side, later; that was freshwater, chlorine bleach and all. Blue. Hurricane wrecked it in the seventies, but it's still under there, with roots dripping from the walls and ceiling. I saw it. Found my way down there, one time, through a tunnel. Diving boards, rats all over the place, hardly any light coming down. It's too damp, all around here, nowhere to sleep."

Scott just smiles, about to say he understands, that he won't be tricked, and then water hits the path, ten feet away. One stream, and then another. Standing on the wall, high above, two young men piss off the edge. Scott cannot make out their faces.

"What?" Ray shouts.

The twin streams waver a little, but keep coming.

"What'd you do if someone came over, whipped it out, and pissed in the middle of your living room?"

"I'd wonder what the fuck kind of place I'm living in!" one of them shouts back. And then—after a few shakes, taking their time zipping up—they are gone.

Ray looks out across the river, then up toward the wall again, muttering. He rebaits his hook, resuming the conversation as if there had been no interruption.

15

"Mayor wants everyone in a shelter, and you know they make you stay in there if you take their food. Makes everyone feel safer, not to see people sleeping on the street, but in the shelter they lock you in and you can't choose who'll be sleeping, who'll be lying awake next to you. Then there's baby-bird syndrome—too much gets given to you, you'll never learn how to care for yourself. You know how it is."

"I don't like you intimidating I'm homeless," Scott says. "I got plenty of places to stay."

"You got a toothbrush sticking out your back pocket," Ray says. He has untied the fishing line from his toe and is winding it around two crossed sticks. "Man, I'm not riding you—that's nothing to be ashamed of. You're kind of sensitive, aren't you? Doesn't matter where you sleep, it's the same all over again. Lonely."

"This is right what I want to be doing," Scott says, "at this point— whatever's next will be building on it. I'll be carrying all this, all my experiences. I got a lot behind me and all sorts of hopes out in front. You listening to me?"

"Obvious," Ray says. He rocks his body forward and farts. "That is obvious."

"That was flat philosophy," Scott says. "You wouldn't know obvious."

Standing, Ray steps into his sandals. He tightens his belt, tucking in the loose end like he is putting a sword in a scabbard. Turning, he steps back toward the stone wall, which is covered in green vines. Scott had not noticed the bicycle leaning there. He watches as Ray untwists a length of wire from the back of it, then returns, picks up the eel, and pierces its mouth with the wire. The eel's body widens and flattens at the end, into a kind of tail; other than that, it looks just like a snake. Ray bends down, then lies on his stomach. He leans over the edge of the walkway and attaches the wire to a metal hook in the concrete, so the eel slips back under the water.

"It'll keep that way," he says, dusting himself off. "Fish won't bother it much. Up here, it's all birds and squirrels."

Scott just nods. He decides to let it go, not to comment on the eel. The old man takes hold of the bicycle again and begins pushing it down the path, toward the circular staircase. Scott follows. He notices the strip of grease marking the inside of Ray's slacks, right at the cuff.

The bicycle has a kind of rack built onto the back, a blue plastic milk crate atop it, bound by wire hangers. Pine tree–shaped air fresheners dangle all over the frame. It's an old-time three-speed, its chain and sprocket free of rust; its tires are bald, but its spokes are straight. Plastic streamers hang from the grips, and one car stereo speaker, oval, is attached to the middle of the handlebars, cord dangling.

At the stairway, Ray stops, then lifts the bicycle over his shoulder.

"I could carry it for you," Scott says.

"No, you couldn't." Ray begins climbing, slowly, around and around.

Scott hesitates, then follows. "In the museum," he says, his neck bent back, his voice carrying upward, "saw a picture of a bicycle with a bull's horns for handlebars. Tail hanging down under the seat."

Ray does not reply. Breathing hard, he climbs without stopping to rest. Sometimes the bicycle rings out against the railing, and then he grunts and adjusts his grip. At the top, he sets it down and stands for a moment, wiping his face with the forearm of his shirt. With his open hand, he pounds the handlebars, to straighten them. The rearview mirrors quiver and settle.

"Where you headed?" Scott says.

"Got some things to take care of before nightfall." Ray pulls a small radio from his pocket and plugs the speaker's cord into it; he fiddles with the dial until music blares out. Violins and piano, working themselves up. He turns it louder, then throws a leg over, straddling the seat. He rests one foot on a pedal, then pushes. The speaker points back

17

toward the seat so the music passes around him and is left behind in his wake.

"Catch you again, sometime," Scott says.

Ray's body sways side to side, pulling away. In a moment, the music is gone; the path curves, and he disappears from sight.

Scott kicks his way through the tangled grass, toward the abandoned buildings. The gate is broken, forced open, and he steps onto the red brick. The windows of the biggest structure are solid plywood; the smaller ones still have glass—it would be too dangerous to sleep in here, where someone could see you from the outside. Scott smiles to himself, thinking how transparent Ray is to him, how obvious it is that the old man sleeps here, somewhere. He has ridden off as a diversion, so he can return later. Scott knows that trick well.

Atop one of the small buildings, a stone woman reclines with a waterwheel; on top of another, a bearded river god is held down by chains. Scott keeps walking along the bricks, parallel to the river and above it. Past the buildings, the bricks beneath his feet turn to blacktop; here and there, thick glass squares, only four inches across, break the surface. Down on his knees, he squints through and can see nothing; he wonders if the swimming pool is under him, rats diving through the water, or if Ray had been having him on, trying to get him to believe a lie.

The walkway leads out to a gazebo that overlooks the river. A low dam, bent at an obtuse angle, stretches to the other side, allowing a constant overflow, a thin white veil of water. On the lip, a metal keg is hung up, thrown into the river from some party upstream. Scott wills it to go over, but it does not. It stays there, spinning, rolling in place.

Since he has been in Philadelphia, he has not covered the miles like he once had, but now he feels he is really traveling, getting somewhere, even more than in those times. All his circling is unwinding inside him. He leans against one of the gazebo's rotten pillars, where someone has scrawled IN LOVING MEMORY OF TINO 1974–1993.

18

Snake

Unzipping his pack, he takes out a jar of baby food, pureed peas and carrots, and eats it with a plastic spoon. He found a whole case of it, barely expired, out behind Pathmark, and took all he could carry. It doesn't taste bad, now that he's used to the texture, and it is healthy, full of vitamins.

The wind ruffles the water. It pushes the sun farther across the horizon and finally off the edge. Dusk begins to spread. He leans against the railing, warm wind blowing hair from his face. Behind him, he knows, the museum looms. Lights are coming on in the tall buildings downtown. He imagines the figure he is cutting, standing alone against this backdrop; he wishes someone were watching him now, standing in front of the city. If they came within earshot, he would tell them that it's possible for a person to change himself. It's a matter of making that decision, then putting it into action.

Four

Advice

Terrell shivers. He wants to untuck his shirt, to whip off his belt, to shout. It is dark in the museum, with hardly any windows, and all those are full of sun; the sun is everywhere outside, where he wants to be. Here, inside, there is no one else his age. The only other black people are the security guards, who either sit on benches, looking bored, or sleepwalk past, radios squawking from their hips.

The rooms go on and on. Underground and up in the air. It is the biggest building Terrell knows, and being inside it is almost as bad as church — church is over, at least for today.

He likes the room of armor, all the swords and spears and the round shields. He likes the black-and-white photographs of naked women. *Nudes*, Ruth said, and had not made him stop looking. Now he passes paintings that are only orange squares, and then endless pictures of flowers. None of this interests him. Boats in the ocean, snow in

20

the mountains, white women in long dresses. Terrell wants to scratch the paint away with his fingernails.

In a corner, though, stands a wooden box, two feet high with a small window on one side. He bends down to see inside, where three metal points have marked lines—red, blue, and black—on a small piece of paper. If anything is moving, it is too slow to tell. Terrell waits, staring inside, trying to figure it out. He jumps a little at the sound of the voice.

"You're probably wondering what that is."

Two cowboy boots point at Terrell, the man standing close. Terrell looks up, into the skinny white face.

"What it is, is you got the red, there, measuring the temperature and humidity, to protect the art. The blue keeps track of seismical activity—earthquakes, even little ones. Tremors."

The man stands too close, his voice just above a whisper. Terrell tries to step back, away, and kicks the wall behind him. The man's blue jacket looks like some sort of costume; he is no taller than Terrell; he smiles as he speaks, and the air between them smells like peppermint.

"Scott," he says. "That's my name. How about you?"

"Eric," Terrell says. "Eric Swan."

"And how old are you, Eric?"

"Thirteen."

"Thirteen," Scott says, rubbing his hands together.

"I didn't ask to talk to you," Terrell says.

"Exactly," Scott says, not even slowing. "If I'm scaring you, you don't have to. You're not frightened of me, are you?"

"What about the black line, then?" Terrell says.

"Now we're having a conversation," Scott says. "You have to like that."

"The black line," Terrell says, standing his ground.

"The black line," Scott says. "That one can detect when a person's lying, like I'm doing right now. See that jump there, the black one?"

"What?"

"Why would I lie to you? I'll tell you why—I'm testing you. You have to test people all the time, to see the edges of a situation, who you can trust. Strangers you just met, even your friends—maybe your friends most of all, since you have to trust them more."

People shuffle around them, pause to stare into paintings, then move away. The skin of Terrell's face feels hot. He does not look at Scott, but past him, over his shoulder, at a painting of a haystack.

"Answer me this," Scott says. "Have you made some real mistakes in the people you've picked as friends?"

"No."

"Go ahead and trust them, then," Scott says. "You'll be sorry."

"Terrell!" Ruth says, suddenly ten feet away. "You come away from there!"

"No reason you had to lie to me about your name," Scott says.

"Machine didn't catch me," Terrell says, moving away. "You would have known."

It seems Scott is following, also stepping toward Ruth, but when Terrell looks back, he is gone.

"Mind yourself," Ruth says. Her face is all twisted, her braids clicking. "Don't you know better than that? Man like that, next thing I know you'll be gone for good. Who knows what that kind of person wants with a boy like you."

"We were just talking," Terrell says, enjoying himself. "He was all right."

"He was not all right."

Terrell walks ahead again, beyond the sound of her voice. Circling from room to room, he looks at the floor, then the ceiling. He is not supposed to get more than one room ahead of her; when he hears her humming grow louder, he moves on. Almost every Sunday, it is this same thing. Ruth only goes to church because she thinks it's good for

22

him, and because she likes to sing. *Jesus set a good example*, she says, *wherever it was he came from*. Terrell doubts that Ruth even likes it here, in the museum; she'll tell the neighbors about it, as if it will impress them.

Most of the rooms are empty, but floorboards creak and voices answer each other, bouncing through doorways. All the air has been sucked in and out by all the people, again and again, every day. Terrell can hardly breathe.

Out in the foyer of the museum, things open up. The ceiling is high, and sun shines in through the row of front doors. His friends are out there, now—close by, probably; it's safer around here than in the neighborhoods, and cooler along the river, in the fountains, on the grass under the bushes. He trusts them; he doesn't have to test them. Terrell smiles, thinking of the man, Scott. Ruth hadn't liked that one bit.

He turns away from the sun and begins climbing the marble steps. At least, in here, he is safe from being laughed at, wearing this shirt with the collar, these pants with creases up the front. These brown shoes used to belong to someone else. Someone with deformed feet.

At the top of the stairs a twenty-foot-tall metal woman stands, naked and green, pulling a bow back, ready to shoot an arrow. If she let go, the string would tweak her nipple. Terrell bends his neck, looking at her, until he hears Ruth at the bottom of the stairs, singing some hymn to herself; then he steps through a stone doorway, into rooms full of crosses, paintings of old people praying. He runs his fingers along the smooth sides of vases big enough to hold him, if he could fit through their necks. The rooms are darker, glass cases lit up. Little men made of pottery. Clay horses.

*   *   *

The whole time he was talking to the boy, Scott's thoughts had been forking out ahead of him. Now he waits upstairs in the Asian wing, ready for Terrell to come along.

Scott has been following him, waiting for the right moment, ever since he saw the woman the boy came in with. She had swung through the front doors, into the foyer, and filled all that space. The ceiling stretched eighty feet overhead and a mobile as big as a row house hung from it, pieces of curved metal twisting from cables. She wore a blue dress, her hips thick and high. Beads in her hair—strings of long, thin braids. Her feet forced into tight white sandals. Scott liked the look of her, the shape of her, like someone you could hold onto at the end of a long day when you were tired, something solid to hold onto while everything else whirled past. He chose the boy because he wanted to meet her; he needs a handhold, an opening. Now the boy is coming closer—his light footsteps, the shuffle of shoes too big for him. Scott waits, hidden.

"Terrell," he says, stepping out from behind a pillar. "Now I know your name."

"So what?" Terrell tries to keep moving, but soon gives up. "You been following me?" he says.

"Just thought we got kind of interrupted by your mother," Scott says, "right when we were getting somewhere. You see, all I was saying back there, that was true, and it got me thinking of a few other things no one told me about, when I was younger. Had to learn it all myself."

"The only reason I talked to you," Terrell says, "the only reason I'm talking to you, is because Ruth—that's my sister, not my mother—doesn't like it, me talking to you. If she sees me doing it, then maybe we'll get to leave early. I never wanted to talk to you."

Scott does not respond, not right away. They stand still for a moment, silent in that space, faded paint on the huge wooden beams above, dull brass fittings on the heavy wardrobes along the wall. Through a doorway, skylights illuminate a bamboo fence, low trees. A

24

teahouse and Buddhist shrine have been taken apart piece by piece, then put back together, brought all the way from Japan. Scott has seen it before, plenty of times.

"Well," he says, "I think that may be true, and it's real clever of you, but I think it's more than that, talking to me. You're trying to prove something to me, and that's cool. It's not like I need you to be afraid of me."

"I'm not."

"But, man, there are givers and there are takers, you know? I'm telling you some things here; this is beyond generosity."

Footsteps draw closer, and Scott waits, silent again. A guard walks into the room, his face in shadow, then goes around them, through another doorway. His footsteps fade.

"Once you get someone talking," Scott says, "then you get to where you know more about them than they know about you. See what I mean? You never want to show someone all the way how smart you are." He smiles, his eyes adjusting to the faint light coming through the latticed screens along the wall.

"You don't know about me," Terrell says. "It's you doing all the talking."

"Exactly," Scott says. "True. But I'm careful about what I say." He pauses, waving his hands toward all the room's corners. "You know why it's so dark in here? Light wears things down, that's why. What are you thinking about?"

"Read a book in school," Terrell says, then stops, as if reconsidering how much he wants to say. "It was about two kids who slept in a museum," he says. "Hid from the guards, every single night. You could do that here."

"I have a place to sleep," Scott says, his voice rising. "Why would I want to do that?"

"I didn't say that."

Scott likes the shape of the boy's face in the half-light—chin jutting out, jaw set, the skull smooth and rounded. He looks into it, and questions return to him, remembered from his interview at the hospital: *Before you were fifteen, did you shoplift? Were you a bully? Bullied? Did you torture or kill animals? Set fire to or destroy things that weren't yours? Would you say you like to see what you can get away with?*

"Goodbye," Terrell says. He turns quickly and struts away, before he can be slowed or stopped.

"Fine," Scott says. He walks in the other direction, not wanting to appear desperate. He does not even look over his shoulder to see if the boy is watching him. In the next room, wooden figures line the walls, their hands missing fingers, their bodies lacking arms, their earlobes stretched out. A dragon writhes across the ceiling, ready to fall on Scott's head.

"What are you smiling about?" the guard says, and Scott has to squint to see him, there in the corner.

"No law against it, is there?"

Two wooden heads sneer angrily, vertical cracks in their faces; they rest on thick columns, making it seem as if their bodies are encased or hidden behind.

"Usually it means someone's trying to get away with something," the guard says.

"Doesn't it make you want to smile back?" Scott says.

"I'm working," the guard says.

It is about time, after all, to return to the heat outside. Admission is free on Sunday mornings, and Scott has been inside almost all day. Nothing straightens him like the colors of the paintings, the cold rooms of statues. Now he walks past the Indian temple hall, stone people balancing the roof on their heads, and then finds one of the side stairways and descends toward the coat check. He feels strong, full of anticipation. A window runs the length of the stairs, and through it he can see the dark water of the Schuylkill, its curves mirrored by the highway. Closer, a forty-foot woman stretches across a billboard wearing a spangled white bathing suit and panty hose, reclining with her blond hair thrown back. He can't make out the words beneath her, nor the letters on the smokestacks spitting up black clouds behind her. Trains come and go into the switching yards at Thirtieth Street Station, heading out only to circle back.

He retrieves his pack from the coat check, then heads outside, onto the museum's front steps. It is late afternoon, still getting hotter. Taking off his jacket, he jams it into the top of his pack. He likes to feel the sun on the skin of his arms.

Straight ahead, towers of glass stretch from the center of the city; to his right, a gilded horseman shines gold, blinding. Scott sits near a small fountain, where black girls play, screaming and splashing each other. Some wear bathing suits and others just T-shirts, their colored underwear showing through. Red, blue, flowered. One little girl leaps up, smiling, and flips her middle finger at her friends. The others laugh.

The sun shines heavily, not letting up; Scott wishes he had a hat. All he wants is to get a good look at the woman. Her name is Ruth. He does not want to talk to or touch her. Not yet. He knows you have to be ready for someone, to make it worth their while. It would be enough to see her in the sun, swinging her hips as she walks, shielding her eyes from the glare. Ruth. If she would only come outside and see him there, look at him, even if it is only a glance, her eyes passing over him, their slight pressure joining the heat of the sun. But too much time has gone by now, and she and the boy must have gone out the back way. Scott has missed her. Standing, he starts away from the fountain. A tour bus stops at the bottom of the steps, and people swarm up and past him, speaking all kinds of words he cannot understand.

Five

☰ Proof

ook at that nigger come," Darnay says, and Terrell and Swan laugh,
watching John walk toward them between the river and the empty
train tracks. The tops of cars are visible, sliding along the Market Street
Bridge, above and behind him.

Terrell knows it's a bad feeling to be the last to arrive, to know the
other three have been together without you, talking where you can't
defend yourself or cut one of them in return. John is closer now, his lips
moving in a silent rap as he approaches, jeans slung low to show the waistband of his underwear. The boys are only thirteen, but they've known
each other for years; they knew John long before he even cared that he's
white. He wears a Phillies cap, sideways and high, so they can see straight
through the mesh, to the gravel path behind him. His hair is reddish, and
his face is a little puffy. Freckled. Reaching out, he slips his palm against
theirs, pulling it smoothly toward him. There's no grip, no slap.

28

"What up?"

"Nothing."

"Got lots to do."

"Word," John says.

Now they're all here, and they look at each other, silent for a moment, uncertain where to begin. The air around them is motionless, hot and damp. Across the river, the train station bakes white in the sun. The boys stand on the strip of gravel and dirt, fifty feet from the fence to the river, the train tracks in the middle. Along the fence, a snarl of bushes and trees hides the parking lot and on-ramp; above, the museum's roof settles against the sky. Things between the four of them feel different, uneasy, everyone growing at different speeds and in different ways. A year ago, Terrell had been the smallest, and now he's as tall as John and Swan. Darnay never stops growing. He speaks first.

"We do the tats," he says, "then the test."

"Dope," John says.

"Dope?" Terrell says. "No one says that anymore."

"What do they say?"

"Not 'dope.' "

"What are we doing here?" Swan says.

Terrell smells his own sweat, feels the hot metal rail through the rubber sole of his shoe. The idea of tests had been Terrell's, though Darnay acts like he thought of it. He takes things over that way. Terrell watches Swan; everyone will have their own test, and Swan's is first. Each will be different.

"Test is set up for four-thirty," Darnay says, and they all look up at the Tastykake billboard, its red-handed clock next to a giant doughnut. It's about a quarter to three.

"I brought the magic marker," Terrell says to Darnay. "You seen this done?"

"Yeah," Darnay says. "No, not really. I heard it described, though,

29

a couple times." He takes the cap off the marker and waves them all closer.

Each boy will get the first letter of his own name, with the rays of the sun around it. First, Darnay draws them on with the marker. He has a few whiskers, like dirt under his chin; he turns his head and there's a *D* shaved into the back. His mother is a hairdresser.

"Let it dry for a second, or it'll smudge," he says.

The tattoos will be on their hips, below their belts, where their parents are least likely to see them—not that their parents are all around, or would care. Swan's foster parents wouldn't ever notice; John's parents would. Darnay could say someone did it to him, held him down. He and Swan live in North Philly, where that kind of thing can happen—being from there gives them some authority, some experience. No one plays on the street up there. They get bused to school, into John and Terrell's neighborhood. Next year, it's high school.

"No one'll see them," Swan is saying. "And that's the point—we'll know they're there. That way we can't be split up."

Darnay reaches into his pocket and drops a handful of matchbooks on the ground. From one, he takes a needle, and begins sharpening it on the sandpaper strip of one of the matchbooks. He touches the needle's point, then sets it aside. He takes four cards of plastic pen refills from his socks—stolen from somewhere—and opens one. A capsule in his fingers, he tries to bite off the top; it explodes, dark blue, all down his arm.

"Just stick the needle in," John says. "Through the plastic."

Darnay nods like that's obvious. His teeth are blue, and he's spitting into the gravel, trying to get the ink out of his mouth.

"I'll go first," he says.

"I'll do it," John says. "I'm down with it."

"That's a pretty big needle," Swan says.

"If it's small," Darnay says, "then you got to stick it in a million times."

30

"It's going to hurt," Terrell says, then catches himself. "That's all right."

"It's supposed to hurt," John says. He sticks the needle into an ink refill, then into Darnay's hip, following the line made by the marker. Darnay—lying on his side, holding down the waistband of his pants— is either smiling or gritting his teeth.

Terrell and Swan watch, though there's not much to see. Above them, a stampede of wild horses, mustangs, fill a Marlboro billboard, the cowboy with his lasso up in the corner. They meet here because it's no-man's-land—no one lives here, near the museum, except old peo- ple who drive straight into the parking garages of the tall apartment buildings, who never really go outside. The boys come here in the summer; sometimes they jump onto the slow-moving trains, then jump off again, lying about how far they've gone. Up the Main Line, or all the way to Trenton. When it's cooler, they play on the rooftops, down near Terrell's house; now the tar is too hot and sticky. It comes off on your shoes, burns your skin.

Swan and Terrell walk away, toward the river. They sit on one of the square cages, full of white rocks, put there to support the bank.

"It's a good idea," Terrell says, looking back at John and Darnay.

"Yeah. It'll be cool, probably."

The river swirls beneath their feet, dark patches of oil like puddles sliding by, rainbows on the surface circling plastic bottles and other trash. Their shoes are untied, thick tongues standing up; Terrell feels the cotton stuffed in the toes of his, to make them fit. He sees that Swan's wearing a pager, transparent orange plastic, attached to the waistband of his shorts.

"Just needs a battery," he says. "Then anyone can call me up, any- time, and I'd know it."

"Lot of people calling you?"

"I wouldn't know."

Terrell's known Eric Swan longer than the others, since second grade—they'd gotten caught taking the pencil sharpener apart, after being told there were razor blades inside. Now Swan is wearing his Sixers uniform. He's so skinny that all the bones in his face show, and that makes his eyes seem larger than they are, switching slowly back and forth. His hair is shaved close, but not as close as Terrell's. Swan's mouth is always set in a slight frown; he's always thinking.

"Didn't you ever want to be the champion of something?" he says. "Have them put a medal around your neck?"

"Champion of what?"

"I don't know. Anything."

Behind them, Darnay's now working on John, who lets out little gasps.

"Sound like my baby sister," Swan calls.

"Don't get in my face because you're nervous."

"I'm not afraid of getting mine," Swan says.

"That's not what I'm talking about," John says.

"Hold still," Darnay says.

Now Swan's staring straight up into the sky. Under Terrell's hand, there's a crack vial between the stones; he flicks it into the water. His keys, on a string around his neck, rattle. He throws a stone at a splintered board floating by, and so does Swan. They both miss. Behind them, two gray-haired white people, wearing red jogging suits, have stopped a short distance from where Darnay is atop John, sticking him with the needle.

"It's fine," John is saying. "We're friends."

After the people walk past, Darnay climbs off. He looks over to Terrell and Swan.

"Your turn," he says.

"Let's see," Swan says.

Darnay and John pull down their waistbands. Both of their hips are covered in ink and blood, smudged all over, the *D* and *J* hard to see.

"We didn't do the rays."

32

"Hurt too much?"

"Takes too long."

"Can add them later, if we want," Darnay says. "Mom's boyfriend got a dragon on his back—took ten times to do it all."

"Mine stands out more," John's saying. "It doesn't look as good."

"Whose fault is that?"

"Not mine."

"Your mother's."

"And your daddy's even whiter. Pasty."

"We supposed to share a needle?"

"That's not about this. Where you been? Health class? Next you'll be handing out condoms."

"That's for Swan to worry about."

"I got one," Swan says.

"They make them that small?"

"Magnum," Swan says, reading the label. "Deal with that." He picks up the needle, then the ink.

"Go with the black," Terrell says. "You'll run out of blue and then it'll be two colors."

"The colors won't show," Darnay says. "It'll just be dark in there."

"Make sure it's deep enough," John says.

Terrell feels the prick of the needle. It hurts less than he feared. A little blood rises up; the wounds will scab over, then heal, the ink caught there beneath his skin's surface. He sits next to a stack of long square railroad ties that stink of creosote. He holds his breath, and so does Swan; they both exhale as Swan puts more ink on the needle.

"How come we're not in the shade?"

"I don't know," Swan says.

The overpass is fifty feet away. They both look toward it, into the shade under it, where an old man is climbing off his bicycle, his head turned, watching them.

"That old dude," Terrell says. "Got nothing better to do."

33

"Don't look at him or he might come over here." Swan starts with the needle again. "You'll have this for a long time. Even when you're old."

"It's not like I'm going to change my name."

"We're getting there," Swan says, and then Terrell just watches the needle go in and out. John drifts closer, then away again; down by the river, he's pulling down his pants enough to check Darnay's work.

Terrell holds still. He thinks of Ruth, wondering about her reaction. It would almost be worth it to see what she'd do, hear the things she'd say. She might just say she's disappointed, close the door to her room, but she might really go off. Ruth will not see it, though—their bathroom door locks, they wear bathrobes, they always knock before entering a room. She does not want him to see her uncovered, so she exaggerates his need for privacy. She could be covered with tattoos, pierced with hoops, branded all over her body and he would not know.

Now Terrell has the needle, working on Swan, slowly pricking the curves of the S. He wonders what Swan is thinking, with that condom in his pocket. Ruth gives Terrell condoms, just leaves them in his sock drawer without saying a thing. He suspects she counts them sometimes, when he isn't there; their number never changes—except for the one he tried on, to see how it worked, if it would fit—and he doesn't know if that makes her worry more or less.

"Better hurry up," Darnay's saying. "Don't want Swan to be late for his date."

"You'll mess it up if you hurry," Swan says.

"We're done," Terrell says.

Hitching up their pants, they squint at the Tastykake clock above. They have twenty minutes to get there, wherever they're going. Terrell drops the needle in the middle of the pile of empty ink refills and matchbooks, lights the whole thing. The boys walk beneath the overpass, past faded spray paint, tired old tags, past the old man; he's now pretending to sleep, with his head propped on his bicycle tire, one long arm wrapped inside the frame. John throws a stone, just misses him. They laugh. The old man shifts a little; his eyes don't open enough to show.

The four boys climb a small hill, onto a level field of grass, where men stand in every shadow, lean against every tree, whistling and sending hand signals. They talk low, calling each other Negro if one ventures from tree to tree. The dealers have to stay put, hold their spots; some days the boys run errands for them—going to buy a cheesesteak or a soda might mean five dollars, even ten. Today there's no time.

Terrell feels the tattoo, rubbing beneath his clothes; he hopes the ink is dry, and the blood, that they won't stain his underwear. He follows Darnay across the road, onto the wide sidewalk in front of the museum, the wide stone steps. Terrell pretends not to notice the man sitting there; he tries to keep walking smooth and easy; he holds the keys in his fist, tight on their string around his neck, so they won't make a sound. It's the man he met in the museum, the week before, the one who started the whole idea of testing your friends. The man sits twenty feet up the steps with his shirt off, wearing dark glasses that hide his eyes. It's impossible to say where he's looking. If he sees Terrell, he doesn't do anything about it.

The boys take the path around the side, past the statue with shells for eyes, beyond the steps, beyond where the man can see. Terrell looks back, once. No one is following. He feels his friends around him. They hardly speak as they head down toward Boathouse Row, where the white boys from the private schools are practicing for the crew season.

"This way," Darnay says, as if they should have known to turn. He's the only one who knows where they're going.

They cross Kelly Drive and follow a smaller road, into Fairmount Park, trees on every side. Terrell is nervous, and he doesn't have to do a thing. Not today, he doesn't. He can't think of what he'd want to be the champion of, and that bothers him. Swan walks to one side; he doesn't look nervous, but he doesn't seem excited, either. He was the only one

35

who would admit he hadn't done it before—no one doubted Darnay, and no one believed John, but they only needed one person for the test, anyway.

Walking faster in the sun, they take their time through the shadows. Single file, then abreast, still not speaking. They all wear unlaced hightops, and they hardly lift their feet, sliding them to keep their shoes on. The four of them move with a slithering sound.

"It's simple," John says. "You just stick it in and move around some."

"I'll remember that," Swan says, and they all laugh, not sure why.

"Your test is next," Terrell says to John. "Don't forget that."

A car rolls by, moving slowly, its windows tinted black. Old mansions show through spaces in the trees and are hidden again. They see baseball fields, the reservoir, basketball courts.

"Play some hoops later, probably," John says, shooting an imaginary ball. He has a court on his driveway, but his mother doesn't like them to play there. She always watches, frowning, from the kitchen window.

"How far we going?" John says.

"She gave me directions," Darnay says. He leads them off the road, onto a narrow path, under the trees. Single file, the boys kick bottles and cans from underfoot.

"People always finding dead bodies in here," Terrell says.

Heat is caught in the bushes, thick in the leaves. Swan sneezes, then sneezes again. Bugs wheel around Terrell's head, mosquitoes fill his ears.

"Who is she?" John says. "What's her name?"

"You don't know her," Darnay says. "She's older than us, friend of my cousin. Name's Lakeesha." He stops walking, then, and turns around. He points at Swan. "You go wait by that dead tree. On this side, so we can see you. She'll come."

"Good luck," Terrell says, and no one laughs like he expected. Their faces are serious.

The three of them watch Swan walk away, and then they climb into the branches of trees—Darnay in one, Terrell and John in another—so they'll have a good view but won't be seen. Terrell hears a car, far away. There's no one around. The palm of his hand smells like metal, from holding the keys. Below, Swan does not look in their direction; he just stands in a spot of sunlight, waiting; he doesn't sit down or lean against the tree. Clouds slide by, close overhead; the shadows they cast are no cooler than the sun. Swan didn't ask why they had to watch, since that was both obvious and complicated. He looks smaller now than he does up close. More like a boy. Terrell thinks he must look that way himself, from a distance.

She comes from the other direction. Lakeesha. Wearing a baseball cap—she's too far away to tell what team—and she's at least as tall as Swan. She says something to him, and he says something back. Turning a circle, she tries to tell if anyone is around; she doesn't see them. She's wearing a backpack that looks like a teddy bear, its legs and arms sticking out.

Without warning, Swan starts taking off his clothes. His shoes and socks, his jersey, his shorts, and his underwear. He's standing there naked next to the girl and all she's done is take off her backpack and put it on the ground. The black ink blotches Swan's hip. His ribs show. His dick is pointing at the trees, the sky.

Terrell thought they might have kissed or something, but there's nothing like that. The girl pushes her shorts down; there's a flash of white underwear inside them. She steps out of the shorts, then sits down on them. She doesn't take off her shirt, her hat, or her sandals. When Swan sits down next to her, she touches his elbow and brings him around until he's kneeling, facing her. Leaning back, using the backpack as a pillow, she pulls Swan down on top of her.

37

The Ambidextrist

Terrell doesn't wish he was in Swan's place, though he no longer fears someone will come down the path, no longer worries about his balance. He does not wish he was anywhere else but here. Mosquitoes land on his legs, his face, and he does not slap at them. He can hear nothing but John's breathing, and his own. The branch cuts his legs; when he shifts his weight, leaves quiver. He sits still again. Behind him, pale and motionless, John hisses to move left, that he can't see. Close by, Darnay just smiles, his teeth still faintly blue.

It's too far to see much—only the smooth skin running down from her waist, over her hips, the thin curve of her thigh. Her hands are down between their legs, and Swan's are on either side of her, holding his chest above hers. His head is turned the other direction—away from her, away from the trees. His bare ass rises up in the air. The girl slaps at it and says something, her mouth close to his ear. She bends her knees, sandals flat on the ground, and his ass comes up again. His legs are stretched out, the light soles of his feet showing. Her hat falls off, her arms stretched lazily to the side; she seems to laugh as she helps Swan again, as they struggle together.

When they're done, they sit next to, not facing, each other. Their mouths are not moving. Swan puts his shoes on barefoot, his socks in his hand. Lakeesha stands and pulls up her shorts in one quick motion. The teddy bear is already on her back. She walks away from Swan as he starts for the trees, stumbling, his shirt halfway over his head.

38

 Six

Beauty

At the pharmaceutical companies, sometimes the drugs are tested on animals first, and other times those tests are simultaneous. At a place like that, they don't know what a person is—not that most of the subjects give them much to think about. It changes you, Scott knows, wears you down. They can search you at any time, and you're never allowed to leave when you want, no visitors, surrounded by drunks and addicts who purge their systems to get in, people who then binge away thousands of dollars in just a few weeks. In the trials, you can only use the pay phones—some say all calls are listened to, recorded—and you can get kicked out, no pay, for even touching another phone. People turn on each other for nothing at all; first there's the slither as someone takes off his belt, and then the slaps and the cries and the air whipped all around. Anyone who tells or complains will be found later, on the outside, where there are no orderlies.

Scott had been willing to put up with all this—and there were always clean sheets, actual mattresses, and hot showers, not to mention the money—until his last trial, which was over a month back. That was where he got crossed.

They'd been testing some kind of cold medicine. He'd gone in with Oliver, an acquaintance he'd met down next to the river. Oliver was experienced, an expert, full of knowledge. Some subjects stole drugs indiscriminately, ending up with bottles of stool softeners or worse, but Oliver knew the prescription names better than a pharmacist. More important, he always knew where the most lucrative trials were, or where they would be.

In that trial they got checked with the tongue depressor and the flashlight after every pill. Only half of the subjects were on the cold medicine—Scott was—and the rest were on the placebo. While he'd been unable to stay awake, those on the placebo, like Oliver, must have been jacked up on some kind of speed. They never slept.

This was back when Scott carried substantial amounts of cash on his body, before he knew better. The company provided lockers for valuables, but no one trusted them. Half awake, fighting to rise, he had found the money gone. Oliver sat in the next bed, staring at him, though the television was on. He denied the accusation before Scott even got it all the way out.

"No, man," he said. "I been watching you the whole time, to make sure nothing like that happened. I only stepped out once or twice, sneaking a smoke, and some fucker must've slipped in then."

That was the end of drug trials for Scott. He disliked the idea of Oliver watching him while he slept, and the likelihood that he'd touched him made it even worse. It was both the money and the principle of the thing, neither one more than the other. Never again will he let himself be locked into a place with friends who aren't friends.

Now, sitting on the steps of the museum, he can only remember this. It's the middle of the day and the sun is straight overhead. There are no shadows. It's not so hard putting up with these temperatures, since it means the nights don't get too cold; he's not yet sure what he'll do once winter returns. Now heat shivers the air, makes it harder to see. He squints. A man sits facing away from him, on a bench at the bottom of the steps. Two girls roller-skate past.

The waist of these pants is cinched in with a safety pin. Once, in the drug trials, they'd been given leather hobby kits, and he'd made a belt—he'd meant to center his name across the back, but had misjudged how skinny he was, so it rode above his right hip. The belt had been stolen with his other pants, a few nights back. These pants are not as good, their hems gone ragged; taking out a match, Scott singes off the loose strings.

He's found a new backpack, but one of the straps is gone and he's replaced it with a piece of twine, doubled back. Next to him, and a step down, his boots stand with the socks draped across their tops. His T-shirt dries on his other side; he reaches for it, flips it over. He's rinsed it in the fountain along with the socks, after his hair. He rakes his bangs back, wanting them to dry right, feathered over his ears. It's important to look good, he knows, if he wants to be treated decently; he has a trial tomorrow, at the hospital, where he won't have to deal with any other subjects, won't be taking any drugs. They'll just be taking pictures of the inside of his head, checking to see what his brain looks like when he puts it in motion.

He has been watching the man at the bottom of the steps for over half an hour now. Plenty of people look alike, and sometimes he has to see someone move, hear them speak, before he is certain. Whether or not this man is Oliver, the similarity has made Scott remember those times. That has made him anxious.

He moves closer, quietly, and it's clear before he gets halfway there. Oliver always wears a stocking cap, regardless of the heat. He is eating a stick of beef jerky, drinking a can of V8, and there's probably some strategy in that—some say drinking four gallons of water the night before will hide a dependency; others drink mineral water or vinegar, eat pounds of raisins and spinach, liver barely cooked. Scott's heard all the tricks, though he doesn't need them; he thinks that's selfish, dishonest. If it throws off the tests, it could hurt someone down the line.

He stands transfixed, twenty feet from Oliver, whose back is still turned. He is about to retreat when Oliver, with a quick jerk, looks over his shoulder.

"Scotty!" he says. "Wondered if that was your ass, sitting up there."

"It was," Scott says. "It is."

"Come on over here."

Oliver wears running shoes with no socks, a tweed vest with nothing underneath it. His age always seems to vary, swinging between forty and sixty; today he looks old. His face is fleshy, and blood vessels line the bridge of his nose.

"Been missing my sidekick," he says.

"Where is he?" Scott says.

"Talking about you, of course. Spare a few bucks?"

"No. How about you?"

"Touché," Oliver says, chuckling. His brow folds down, almost hiding his eyes. The stocking cap is brown, a white stripe around it. "Haven't seen you around the trials," he says. "You haven't done something stupid like getting a job, have you?"

"Nothing like that," Scott says. He takes off his sunglasses, rubs the lenses on his pant leg, then puts them back on. What frustrates him most is he can't prove Oliver crossed him, though they both know what happened. That knowledge is in the tone of Oliver's voice.

"Word is there's real money in St. Louis," he's saying, "and four thousand a month down in Baltimore." He tears the jerky with his teeth, talks as he chews. "Play pool, watch movies, eat free food."

"That's not for me," Scott says.

"Networking," Oliver says. "Some of these trials I'm talking here haven't even been posted. What's your problem?"

"I'm tired of moving all the time, is what it is. Feel like staying in one place for a while."

"And you picked this one?" Oliver says. "Sometimes, though, sometimes I almost know what you mean. Right now, for instance, I got a woman in a place over on Market Street."

Scott yawns to show Oliver how impressed he is.

"One quarter at a time, I admit that, but she knows I'm there, she talks to me."

"Pathetic," Scott says.

"Scotty, Scotty." Oliver crushes the V8 can in his fist. "I got to love your high horse. Missed it. You know, we're going to have a little get-together tonight, little party. You might do a little better for yourself if you mingled more. Could make it easier on yourself."

"Never said I wanted it easy."

"You've got to come down a little, is all," Oliver says. "Or some-one'll bring you down."

A cheap metal ringing sounds, and then the bicycle clatters by— horns and flashlights lashed to the handlebars, music blaring from the single speaker, a tangle of wire bending and recoiling over the back wheel. The old man's legs spin as he sits rigid, churning past, not even glancing at Scott.

"Wow," Oliver says.

"Have to talk to that guy," Scott says, turning away.

"Hold on," Oliver says, "I'm not through with you." But Scott's already gone.

Vaulting up the steps, he jams his feet into his socks, then his boots. His damp shirt in one hand, he throws his pack over his shoul-der. Stumbling, he picks up speed as he heads along the paved path, around the side of the museum. He meant to follow only beyond where Oliver can see, to escape him; then he sees Ray—fifty feet away, stopped, not looking back; he begins to ride again, unsteady until his balance finds its speed.

Scott doesn't stop running. He rocks from one leg to the next on the heels of his boots, passing joggers, almost tangled in the leashes of dogs. He's not sure why he's following, but he doesn't want Ray to escape, to believe he's put one over.

"Whoa there, cowboy," someone says.

The twine cuts into his armpit, and still he runs. He hears voices, music, on Ray's radio; classical music floats back like a soundtrack to his pursuit. When he doesn't feel he can run any more, he lets momentum take over; he forgets about stopping. Past boys carrying long oars, around women with baby carriages. Ray could lose him if he wanted to, and Scott suspects he's visible in the bicycle's rearview mirrors. He suspects the old man is leading him somewhere. If he is not catching Ray, he is at least falling no farther behind. His curiosity grows with every step.

Then Ray rides straight across the brick border, clattering and weaving through the two-way traffic on Kelly Drive. Scott follows— cars honk and swerve around him—into the park, onto a small side road, under the trees. And it's not long before the old man leaves the road altogether and heads straight into the woods.

Scott crashes down the path after him, unable to see him any longer, and finally slows—no reason to rush if he gets headed in the wrong direction, and he doesn't want to overtake Ray, either. He keeps moving along the path, his skin gone from slick to cool, leaves slipping along his arms, his ribs. He'd slept out here once, built a lean-to from a couple of pallets; he'd still felt exposed.

Out in the west, he'd seen spray paint on trees and been told it was the mark of loggers, choosing which ones they'd take. Here it serves no purpose, but blue and yellow lines, initials mark the trunks. The bicycle's trail is one line in the dirt, sometimes splitting in two and then coming back together where the rear tire followed the front. Ray's pushing it now, his footprints on the left.

And here the old man has left the path—leaves are overturned, showing their colors, not their burned-out, dusty sides. Here, the bicycle's pedal has scored the bark from a tree trunk. Scott follows. The sun clips by, through the leaves. A spot off to the left shimmers for an instant, in the corner of his eye—behind him, down in the bushes. For a moment, he fears the old man has crashed; leaning down, he sees it's only that the bicycle has been stashed there, back under the foliage. He smells the dirt, the dry leaves, a hint of cinders in the back of his throat. Twenty feet away, he sees a gap in the brush. That's where the old man has gone. He's close.

Their branches growing together, up high, the bushes form a kind of tunnel. Scott pauses; he doesn't know what he expects Ray to be doing when he finds him, whether he'll be waiting or setting an ambush. Scott moves slowly, into the tunnel of leaves and twigs. Fishing line, weighed by little round bells, hangs here and there; he slips by without touching them, muffles the bells in his fists. Halfway in, afraid of leaving footprints, he takes off his boots and socks and carries them.

A light shines from the ground. A round pond, water reflecting, the brightness torn only by the shadows of leaves. Scott stands perfectly still, hardly breathing, moving only his eyes. What he sees makes no sense at all, and that intrigues him.

One chair sits at the far end of the pond, and the whole area is only five feet wide, ten feet long, bordered by refrigerator shelving sunk into the ground like a miniature fence. Everything is packed so tightly it's only possible to walk along the edge.

Close to him, flat stones have faces painted on them, eyes and mouths the colors of fingernail polish. Spoons stand, their handles stuck in the dirt, and photographs of faces have been cut from magazines and affixed to their other ends; actresses and sports stars smile, their colors faded. Plastic flowers rise among the spoons, the tiny faces stuck inside the blossoms, encircled by petals. Across the pond, the limbs of dolls and mannequins jut from the dirt, as if their bodies lie below and are about to surface.

The ground has been pounded, polished, so it is smooth and shiny. Scott balances along the edge, nearer the chair. Broken glass spins colored patterns, twisting with keys and bottle caps, marbles, pieces of brick, all embedded in the burnished dirt.

The chair's splayed legs are sunk into the ground; it was clearly once a rocking chair, but now its runners are gone. Scott sits, rests his bare feet in the grooves Ray's have made. He doesn't know whether Ray is hidden, watching him, and he's not certain if that would make him take less pleasure or more from the garden.

Light gathers. At his feet lie tiny human-looking skeletons, built from chicken bones. Lizards and lions, carved from wood and plastic, ring the pond, as if coming to get a drink. Horses and monkeys and elephants, only inches high. Black plastic garbage bags line the pond's bottom, weighed down with stones. The old man must lug buckets up here to keep it full. Scott looks over the garden and wonders about Ray. This is hours and hours of work. Days and weeks and months. And for what? The only answer he can think of is this: because it's beautiful.

Seven

Observations and Pursuits

Ray only passes through the woods to get to his garden, yet he knows them well, travels easily and quietly. He carries his knife in its leather scabbard, inside his pocket, so it will not cut him. His bike hidden, he moves more slowly than he used to; his joints are not accustomed to the jolts and jerks of walking. Overhead, the boughs of trees slide sideways through the air. He is not alone today, he can feel it.

Sometimes when he hears voices he hides for no reason, listens to passing hikers' conversations; he unsheathes his knife and stands still, careful that the glistening of the blade does not give him away. Other times he startles animals—possums and skunks, whole clusters of deer. There are too many deer in the park, he's read about it in the newspaper. Some people want sharpshooters brought in, to thin the numbers; others argue for birth control, darts full of hormones. Packs of dogs—neighborhood, feral, or both, he does not know—chase the deer, yip-

47

ping and howling, crashing through the underbrush. Sometimes he sits in his garden and listens, hoping they'll pass around him, that they won't all rail straight over, destroying his work in the sharpness of hooves and snap of jaws.

Today the woods are quiet. The deer hide somewhere, shivering in anticipation, blackflies lining their hides while the dogs move in arcs and circles, snouts to the ground. Ray walks. He hears no voices, but feels their presence on his skin, a tightening like static.

Then he sees them. Three boys, the white one in the back, all up in the trees. He has been expecting them, patiently drawing them in. He likes the looks of them, young and flexible, yet he wishes they would move; he wants to see the sinews of their arms as they swing from branches, as they struggle to pull themselves upward. He wishes he could see well enough, that he was close enough to see the expressions on their faces.

Ray pulls the shirt up over his chin, afraid they will see his white beard, but they are oblivious to his presence, their attention riveted elsewhere. His breath, hot and moist, collects against his chest as he circles around in the direction their faces point, eager to see what it is they're watching.

Silently, he drops to his hands and knees, burrowing under the bushes, sharp edges brushing the skin of his face, sliding over his eyes. He eases the last thin branches to the side, so he can see into the small clearing, where sun lights the grass.

He is only ten feet from the two of them. He can hear their breathing, the low slap of their skin. The boy's round head seems too heavy for his thin neck to hold like that, parallel to the ground, and Ray watches the curved back of his rib cage, right there under the skin, the girl's lucky fingers finding the grooves between them. The boy jerks clumsily, he doesn't know what he's doing; he slips out, and she helps him back in. Ray appreciates their clumsiness, and the dimples high on the boy's smooth ass, the long muscles running the length of his thighs, tightening into his buttocks, balls swinging out of rhythm, and his fragile shoulder blades, swooping away, cutting back.

Ray realizes his own hips are going now, grinding his pelvis into the ground as all the blood rushes away from his head, filling him up. He stops, fearing that he will make a noise, that he will shake the bushes and betray himself. The boy and girl are finished now, disentangling and clambering apart. Ray slides himself backward, then crawls down the path, hurrying, only his toes and the palms of his hands touching the ground.

As he heads back toward his bicycle, he imagines the two of them—almost dressed now, standing there embarrassed of each other and themselves. He thinks of the boys in the trees; they are probably not dangerous to him, not yet, probably not dealing or using, though danger gets younger every day. He'd like to lead them to his garden, when the chance comes, to show what he's made for them. He pulls his bicycle upright, out from under a bush, and pushes it out of the trees, into the sunlight. He begins to ride.

Sometimes he fantasizes about walking along, holding hands with a boy on each side, or sitting with them on a low stone wall, feet hanging down and their heads resting against his shoulders, their mouths full of questions. It's always boys—little girls look too old these days, their faces those of women, their eyes too knowing. He'd take a boy, every time, like now, when he'd like to have one sitting on the handlebars, every vertebra of his spine within reach, light shining through the thin skin of his ears, legs dangling as he holds his feet out, clear of the spokes.

Ray's leg kicks straight, a tremor rising without warning, and he reins it in, finds the pedal, veers without crashing. He plugs the speaker cord into the radio in his pocket, and a woman's voice talks about the weather. It's been hot, it is hot, it will be hot; there's always a chance of rain. His bicycle rattles above her voice, and people turn to

49

watch him pass. He coasts under a bridge, sees the silhouette of the zoo across the river.

Near the fountain, he dismounts, switching off the radio as the news begins. He's already read the paper, like he does every day, every section he can find. He reads books, too, checked out of the Free Library. Lately it's been Jack London, who's good for the summer. It cools him down. Another winter has passed—they didn't find him stiff one morning, he'd awakened half limber every day—and another is coming. In the winter he reads Louis L'Amour, stories about deserts, novels set in jungles. He only reads books that boys would like, so he can tell them the stories, if he ever has the chance. The boys must come to him—that is his rule; he can only pursue them within reason. He can watch them, but he cannot touch them, unless they ask him to. When they come, he will be ready.

The area around the waterworks is deserted; a few people shuffle from shadow to shadow, conspicuously minding their own business. It's all so familiar to him—he'd sense it if something wasn't right. Still, he looks both ways before slipping through his hole in the fence, easing his bike ahead of him. Then he loosens the broken lock and steps inside the engine house.

Dust motes fill the shafts of sunlight; he knows the air in the dark shadows is no cleaner. Standing still, he listens. There's nothing but the wings of birds, brushing the walls and ceilings. It often takes them a while to find the way back out.

He leans an old piece of plywood over his bike, then drapes a scrap of chain-link fence across the opening, hiding it from view. Graffiti circles the engine house, scrawled around the two-foot holes where water once passed. Boasts have been sent into the future, to people unknown. They do not impress Ray; he doesn't even read them. He's thinking of what he saw in the woods, the good fortune of his discovery. He plays it back in his mind.

50

Observations and Pursuits

*　*　*

Once, Scott had taken part in a test where he wore glasses that made the world appear upside down. After a day, his mind adjusted, and everything seemed normal through the glasses; when he took them off, it was another day before his vision sorted itself out. In the periods between, he caught only glimpses of the world, trying to right itself. He has that sense again now, a little—being in the garden has shifted the way he sees everything outside it. Still, he walks toward the water-works with as much certainty as if the old man had trailed a string behind him.

It's rush hour now, and the sound of the cars on the freeway carries across the river. Scott wishes it was quiet. The two pieces of the gate are buckled sideways, falling in opposite directions; he slides under the rusted chain that joins them, through the low, open triangle. He sees no sign of Ray, nor of the bicycle. The door to the large building is ajar, the chain a decoy, the lock set together, only appearing whole. He lets himself inside.

He hears no motion, no footsteps, on the gritty floor; there is only breathing, rhythmic and close. Scott stands still until his eyes become accustomed, and then the image rises before him.

The old man kneels on the floor, his belt undone and zipper down. His right hand jerks toward the floor, then the ceiling, his left hand down the back of his pants. His head tilts around, his neck slightly twisted. His eyes come open and he sees Scott standing there, watching.

"What?" he says. "Nothing to be ashamed of."

"Didn't say it was," Scott says. "Keep doing what you're doing." Turning, he goes back out the door he'd entered, leaving Ray behind.

He walks away from the waterworks, along the river. At least, he thinks, the old man had not been set upon by the boys, out in the

51

woods. Scott had come across the boys, their faces guilty and spooked; he'd hardly raised his arms into a jujitsu pose, just kidding them, and they'd taken off in the other direction. He hadn't said a word. *Terrell,* he'd wanted to say, but he hadn't remembered the boy's name in time. The way they acted, the way they ran, made Scott want to find Ray. He's been a boy, and he knows they're capable of anything; at that age, all cruelty is entertainment.

He kicks through dead leaves and trash, unable to see his feet. Beneath the overpass, three rats emerge from a pipe, their backs striped orange with rust. The sun is lower now. Trees tilt at angles over the river, their roots loosened by the tides.

Taking a plastic bag from his backpack, he rinses it in the river, then begins picking blackberries from the bushes along the tracks. He tries one and it's sour and juicy, full of grit from passing trains. The empty tracks curve toward a tunnel, under the museum, past where someone has built a shelter from a tree branch and a blue plastic tarp. When the bag is almost full, he pours water in and shakes it, so the dirt settles to the bottom.

Aimless, he has nowhere to be, only the test at the hospital, and that's two days away. He walks back toward the waterworks, and Ray is outside now, smoking, sitting on the balustrade high above the river.

"Where's your bike?" Scott says.

"None of your business."

"That's hardly a bike, anymore. Some kind of contraption. Conglomeration."

"What?"

"Vocabulary," Scott says. "Used to have a calendar gave me a new word every day. Now I always have the right one." He's closer now; he offers the bag to Ray, who takes a berry.

"All you're talking there is a collection of words," Ray says. "And riding beats walking. Lengthens your days."

They sit with the blackberries between them. The sun marks a red line on the river. Some cars have their headlights on, and some do not. Scott wants to ask Ray about the garden, but he is afraid the old man won't answer him. It feels like the kind of thing a person has to offer without being asked.

"Well," Ray says, pointing at Scott's T-shirt, "got to know when to hold 'em, know when to fold 'em. Know when to walk away, know when to run."

"Kenny Rogers is a friend of mine," Scott says. "I worked for him."

"I believe that," Ray says, slapping his leg.

"Got him things," Scott says. "Water, snacks, whatever. One time I even helped set up the lights. Mostly security—that's what I'd call it."

"Those are the smallest cowboy boots I've ever seen," Ray says.

"Had a hat, but it got stolen," Scott says. "Heels like these, by the way, that's for riding horses."

"Spend a lot of time on horseback?"

"It's frustrating," Scott says, "how the only Kenny Rogers song anyone knows is 'The Gambler,' since there's so many better ones. I mean, you got 'Lady,' which is a love song, then one like 'Coward of the County'—that one will teach you as much or more than 'The Gambler,' easy."

"So what?" Ray says.

"I'll tell you this," Scott says. "Horses are one mean animal. Those ears get pulled back, and then watch out."

"Where you going with this?" Ray says, lighting another cigarette. "Way you talk, it cracks me up."

Scott just smiles. He knows how it is to get someone talking fast in a conversation, untethered, until they can't hide themselves. He knows he's getting somewhere.

"So," he says. "What do you think about when you, you know?"

"When I what?"

"When you, what you were doing back there."

53

"What do I think about when I jack off?"

"Or who?" Scott says. "Those roller-skating girls in the tight shorts?"

"No," Ray says. "Not them. That wouldn't be right. I guess I think about my wife—she passed on, some time ago—and all the times I knew her, all the ages, things like that, other things."

"I see," Scott says. "I'll take your word on that." His stomach is unsettled from the berries, but he doesn't stop eating them.

"How about you?" Ray says. "Who do you think about?"

"I don't do that kind of thing, myself," Scott says. When Ray laughs, he does, too.

"Thought you were going to join me," Ray says.

"No, I wasn't," Scott says, stopping his laughter. "What it is, is I don't think about anyone. I just do it, and I think about things."

"Like what? Now we're both lying."

"The sky, some flowers, something like that."

"Bullshit," Ray says.

"If I ever think of someone," Scott says, "I just make them up. If you do it and think about someone you know, that means it'll never happen in real life, between you and that person. That's how it works."

"You even got someone?"

"Well, I got a woman I'm thinking on," Scott says. "It's early, yet. I mean, I know who she is, and where she lives. Hope to do a little research first, so I don't have to go in cold. I've been through some hard times, that way."

Ray just whistles, nodding. He fiddles with a black plastic radio, using a nail file as a screwdriver. His fingers twitch and his hands jerk away; he waits for the tremor to pass, then continues. All the shadows have collapsed into the river, and it slides by, thick and dark, below. Scott watches. He is thinking of everything anyone else has said to him lately, how every line is usually an attempt to end the conversation.

54

Not Ray. The old man is not trying to get somewhere else, despite his tone; he doesn't want to be speaking to anyone else.

"Most people see kindness as weakness," Ray says. "Even you, last time we talked, you were all suspicion yourself, over that damn eel—which was delicious, by the way."

"Right," Scott says.

"Where you going to sleep tonight?"

"Place I have."

"You can stay here, if you want," Ray says.

"I'll take that into consideration."

"Not that I trust you; I mean I can to some extent, but still. Some people will cross you over little things, right away, and others will wait, try to win your trust so you'll open up, show them something bigger to take."

"Tell me something I don't know," Scott says. "I'm out here just the same as you, aren't I?"

"Not the same," Ray says, "since I have a clue. You—you I see out here, kicking and punching some invisible enemy, screaming like someone's twisting your dick."

"You seen that?" Scott says. "Gives everyone a good idea what to expect if they want to tangle with me."

"Out here," Ray says, "sometimes you'll meet someone you can get along with, someone you're happy to run into, and then they'll just disappear and you'll never see them again. The real assholes, though, they never disappear like that."

"I'm not disappearing," Scott says. "What does that say?"

"You really got a place to stay?"

"Yeah, but maybe I'll just take a look in there, see what kind of setup you've got."

It's darker now; Scott hears voices off behind them, but can see no one. He follows Ray back through the fence, into the waterworks.

55

"Engine house," Ray says, his low voice echoing. "Dormers above us, for workmen, but the metal staircases got sold for scrap, along with the engines."

"There bats in here?" Scott says.

"I've never seen one," Ray says. "Sounds like them, sometimes, but I never seen one." Reaching into a hole in the wall, he takes out a roll of foam rubber, flattens it atop a piece of cardboard. "Here," he says. He sits down and slips off his shoes.

Scott sits on the floor, then on the foam, when he sees there's room.

"Now you can tell me some things," Ray says.

"Like what?" He can only see Ray's silhouette, feel his body close in the darkness.

"Why'd you come here, to Philly?"

"To find somebody," Scott says. "That's all. I could tell you why I left where I was, but that might be too sad for you."

"Tell it," Ray says.

Scott lets himself slowly stretch out; the mat is narrow, but they both fit on it, their shoulders not quite touching. Scott's feet are on the foam, while Ray's stick over the edge. The old man will fall asleep first, Scott believes, and then he'll leave, head out to one of his own places. Before then, perhaps, Ray will get tired enough that he'll speak of the garden.

"Well," Scott says. "It wasn't something I did by myself. It was with Chrissie, this girl I knew."

"Girlfriend of yours?"

"I guess so, in a way."

"She was or she wasn't."

"She was beautiful," Scott says. "Her hair was red, bright red, in curls, and she'd be quiet for hours and then say something out of nowhere that was beyond anything. Ignore you a whole day, then say something where you realize she'd been watching you the whole time."

"Either it was right or it wasn't," Ray says. "If you really care for someone, you know, eventually they'll feel the same way, if you pursue them right, if it's supposed to happen."

"Crimes," Scott says. "I committed some crimes." He hears wings in the darkness above, and tries to lie as flat as possible, tries to keep his hands out of the air as he talks.

"This was somewhere in Minnesota, or some Dakota, and we were out of money, hitchhiking west. We'd planned it out perfectly, the two of us—went through it like a dress rehearsal, in a park, the grass frozen under the jungle gym, the swings taken down for the winter.

"The 7-Eleven was empty, except for the clerk. I pretended I didn't know Chrissie at all, came in minutes after her. This would have worked a hundred times out of a hundred, she was so good. She went down to the floor, screaming like the baby was coming. The glass refrigerator windows behind her were all white with bottles of milk. Man. When the clerk left the counter, I leapt back there. Left the cash register alone, figuring it wasn't worth it, especially since the little door was swinging open there below it, all the lottery tickets unguarded. I took those—a round disc of tickets a foot across, striped with colors, LOTTO stamped on every one—and slid them right into my jacket. Thousands of tickets.

"We got out of there clean, beyond that—the clerk was still worrying about Chrissie, asking if she needed anything, and she got us some free hot dogs, a whole gallon of milk, ten dollars in cash. There we were, walking out with all those tickets, every chance in the world."

Ray lies still for a few moments, staring into the darkness as if watching the end of the story disappear from sight. Then he regards Scott for a few moments, squinting, their faces close together.

"So what's so sad about that?" The rough silhouette of his beard changes the shape of his head when he speaks.

57

The Ambidextrist

"It just is," Scott says. He rests on his side, his eyes closed. He can feel Ray's breath, warm on the nape of his neck. Wings shuffle overhead. He will not tell how the lottery tickets were blank, unmarked, worthless. He'd taken that as a sign — that there was no getting ahead by going crooked, not for him, no good luck like that, waiting to change. He does not tell Ray the end of the story, all that happened after the tickets, everything that went wrong with Chrissie. If he said those words, he would have to listen to them himself.

── Eight
═ Neighborhood

O nce, in the house on Kater Street, Ruth would get shocked just turning on the light switches—her hand slapped back over her head, her body suddenly in the middle of the room. She has rewired the whole house, since then; pried out the drywall, drilled holes in the studs, snaked all the wire through. She crawled across the attic to get the ceiling light fixtures, coughing, arms and legs itching from the insulation. Her eyes were stuck shut when she awakened the next morning.

Now that is done, yet it is only the beginning. The pipes in the basement are still wrapped thick with asbestos, and the paint in every room is full of lead—that explains plenty; sometimes, the way Terrell acts, it seems he must have grown up licking the walls.

Terrell's cereal bowl rests in the sink. From the cassette player on the counter, Joan Armatrading is singing about riding tall in the saddle. Ruth runs the faucet so water fills the bowl, so the cereal won't dry and stick. She doesn't know where Terrell goes these days, only that this will be his last summer without a job of some kind; he's reached the age where free time is a danger, a liability. Around adults, the boy cannot sit still, his eyes jerking, feet twitching as if he wants to run for cover. How he acts with his friends, she does not know.

Two dents mark the linoleum, right in front of the sink. This is where her mother stood, so many hours—Terrell's mother, too, who passed on the year after Terrell was born. Cancer. She had been a policewoman, though she worked behind a desk, not out on the street. Her job had been the steadiest in the house. When she died, Ruth was twenty-one.

Their father had gone back to his family after that—down South, to Roanoke, Virginia—and he said it was only to straighten some things out, but he never came back. Cancer, again, Ruth had heard. Now she turns and walks through the doorway, into the narrow living room. On the mantel stands her mother's pottery bust of Nefertiti, surrounded by pictures of her mother and father, some of the two of them with Ruth, none with Terrell. Her father's dirty fingerprints still mark the lampshade, where he tilted it to cast more light on whatever Civil War book he was reading. She cannot bring herself to wipe off those fingerprints, and the whole house is this way; she seeks the balance of saving memories while at the same time not letting the rooms fall to pieces and come down around her. It seems every third house on Kater Street is boarded up, abandoned, condemned—at least she has kept it from descending that far.

Lifting one corner of the blinds, she looks at her father's rosebushes, twisted and overgrown in the yard. Red-and-yellow flowers bloom here and there as the bushes tangle below, sticking each other with their thorns. The day is hot already, dark. Like yesterday, the sun will never shine; it will be so humid it won't even have to rain.

Across the street, Ruth sees some movement in an upper window. She thinks she does. The window is bare, the house abandoned; it seems plywood has always filled that space before, though she is not certain. She lets go of the blinds, then checks herself in the full-length mirror that hangs by the front door. Beads weigh the tips of her braids. Other women sometimes whisper behind her; she hears the words *weave* and *extensions*, but lies can't touch her. In her ears, she wears gold earrings, an X and an O in each one. She is careful of their order, ever since Terrell laughed one morning, threatening to use Ox as her nickname. Ruth knows she will never be a skinny woman, and most days she doesn't even want to be one. She fills her uniform—the gray slacks, white shirt, and burgundy tie, the navy blazer with a gold patch that's supposed to look like a badge. Ridiculous. She's been thirty-four for three weeks, and she wishes she felt that young.

Standing in the open doorway, heat rushing around her, she sees the plywood over the first-floor window, just across the street, bend outward. First one foot, then the other—the cuff of one pant leg snagged and sliding up, revealing a skinny white leg—then a body writhes loose. She takes him for a boy, at first, but the stiff way he walks makes it clear he's a man, barely awake. He slaps his face with both hands, rolls his neck. He rakes his fingers through his hair, feathers it, then pats the sides of his head.

Ruth steps back into the house and closes the door. She draws in a deep breath and holds it. In a few minutes, the street will be clear; she can wait, she has the time. Taking out her lipstick, she leans close to the mirror and redoes her mouth. This isn't really out of the ordinary, she tells herself, but it is a sign, once people start in on a neighborhood. They'd smoke crack, sneak around at all hours, tell their friends, and the police could drive them off but never keep them from returning.

Ruth looks through the peephole and no one is there, nothing is moving outside. When she opens the door, the man is standing ten feet away, on the sidewalk, his hand on top of her gate. He is smiling so widely it looks like it must hurt his jaw. She turns and locks both dead bolts; she feels him watching her.

61

"All these bushes and thorns," he says. "It's like some kind of fairy tale—some prince has got to cut right through here."

Ruth will not be forced back into the house, not again. She steps down, walks halfway to the gate, and then stops, five feet from him. He wears a T-shirt that says KENNY ROGERS WORLD TOUR across the front; the pack on his back is overflowing.

"Saw you're squatting in that house there," she says. "Better think twice about that."

"You got me mixed up with someone else." He stands below her, a few steps down, squinting, the sun catching him right in the face.

"I could call the police," she says.

"You live here?" he says. "This your house?" He looks past her, at the number on the door, his lips moving silently. Memorizing.

"No," she says. "I'm watering some plants for a friend."

"So your friend's out of town?"

"He's coming back today."

"I see," the man says. "Thing is, let's say you do call the police—all they're going to do is take up four hours of your morning, just to tell you this is a misunderstanding. Mistaken identity." He adjusts the sweatbands at his wrists; they are clearly cut from the tops of a pair of tube socks. "Do I look familiar to you?" he says.

"I don't think so," Ruth says.

"You might have seen me before."

"That would explain it, if you did look familiar."

"Saw you checking these out," he says, holding up his hands. "Keeps the sweat from getting on your fingers, wrecking your grip. This way, I can't get shook off." The whole time he talks, he never stops smiling, and he switches which hand he rests on the gate, showing her his left profile, then his right, squaring his shoulders.

Ruth takes another step toward the gate, then stops when he begins reaching into his pocket. She can't tell what's in his hand, and then he puts on the sunglasses. They are too large, covering half his face, making him look like a sharp-chinned insect. She doesn't know if it makes her feel better or worse, being unable to see his eyes.

He lifts his hand when she pushes the gate open. She has to step close to him, down to the sidewalk; it surprises her that she is at least three inches taller, so much bigger—of course, size and strength don't matter much anymore, with everyone carrying some kind of weapon.

As she starts down the sidewalk, he walks beside her. For some reason, there is no one else on the street; she has never seen it so vacant. It seems a car is going to pass, and then it turns, without signaling, at the stop sign. She keeps moving, the man slightly behind her, to one side, his cowboy boots cutting into the corner of her vision.

"What do you got going on today?" he says.

"I'm on my way to work. I don't have time."

"Listen," he says. "Sorry. I feel like we haven't started out too strong, here. Call me Scott. I was just thinking maybe we could get together sometime. Maybe later, when you do have time. We could go out dancing. Even a walk, something simple like that."

"I got a man," Ruth says. "And I've had just about enough."

"A man," he says. "I bet he's nothing like me."

"That's right," she says. They are nearing South Street, where there will be traffic; she grows bolder. "And even if I didn't have someone," she says, "what use would I have for a skinny white boy like you?"

"This is a racial thing, then?" he says. "Let me tell you, now—I'm not caught up in all that. People are people to me, no matter what color."

"That just shows how ignorant you are," Ruth says.

They walk in silence, turning onto South Street, beginning the slow climb to the bridge across the Schuylkill.

"I seen places where there's houses abandoned," he says, "where the city puts false fronts on, to disguise it, just like a wild west town."

"You'd know," she says. "Abandoned houses."

"You can take some cheap shots, Ruth, if you want to," he says, "if it makes you feel better. None of that's going to touch me. If you knew me at all, you wouldn't say that." He licks his thumb, then bends one leg up to rub out a scuff on his boot, struggling not to fall farther behind. When he speaks again, his voice is lower. "You know, sometimes they just take a bulldozer and push a house in on itself, right into its own basement; sometimes they'll just seal up the windows and pump a whole house full of concrete, so no one can go in there."

"I didn't tell you my name," she says.

"How do I know it?" Scott says. "That's easy. That's no mystery. I'm a friend of Terrell's, that's how—met him at the museum, couple weeks back. Even saw you there; thought maybe you saw me."

Ruth does not like this kind of coincidence, if that's what it is. Sometimes she wears headphones, the cord snaking into her pocket, connected to nothing; that keeps people from talking to her on the street, on the train. She doubts headphones would be enough, this morning. Scott had not exaggerated about his grip; each time she believes she's pried him off, it turns out he'd only been buying time to take hold another way.

"Where's your parents?" he is saying. "How about Terrell's?"

"They passed on," she says. "Cancer."

"Know how that is," he says.

Ruth feels the sweat on her back, under her arms, beneath her shirt. She's been walking faster than she usually does, trying to at least shorten the time they'll be alone together.

The bridge passes over two parallel tracks, for freight trains, before it spans the river. She looks over the railing and sees two men below, one walking on each track. They are both white; one seems to be wearing nothing but a blanket; one drags a tree branch behind him. Without warning, as if they feel her gaze, they look upward.

"Scott!" one shouts, dropping the tree branch. "Scott! Dude! Hold up, my man!"

Neighborhood

"Let's keep moving," Scott says.

"They seem to know you." Ruth stands still, enjoying his discomfort.

"I don't hang out with them down there," he says. He's stepped away from the railing.

"Scott!" the man shouts. "It's me, Oliver!"

"Why is that?" Ruth says. "You too proud?"

"Yes, I am," he says. "If I wasn't, I'd be living like that. That's repellent."

"I have to get to work," she says, walking again.

"So do I."

Scott shuffles ahead, catching up only to gradually lose ground, then shuffles ahead again. The arms of a blue jacket stretch from his pack, dangling, bouncing along as if attached to a deflated person. Someone has thrown a shopping cart off the bridge, and it is hung up in the branches of a tree, twenty feet off the ground. The tree branches also stretch down, under the surface of the river, bent by the thick water, hooking shreds of plastic bags, half-sunken cardboard boxes.

"You might be wondering about my job," Scott says. "Right now I'm working over at the drug companies, some, and up here at the university hospital. Working to fight cancer and all. I'm part of the fight against all that."

Ruth does not respond; she does not know why she slipped up and mentioned her parents. Now he is using that information against her, trying to. They wait for the light, so they can cross the on-ramp; they're now over Interstate 76, almost to the station.

"I don't believe you," she says.

Scott just looks over the edge, at all the cars slipping beneath them. He pushes up his sunglasses and smiles.

"Ever cut, burned, or scratched yourself on purpose?" he says.

"Where you coming up with that?"

"Just a question I wanted to ask you. No offense."

They cross the on-ramp.

"How about this one," he says. "True or false. When I get bored I like to stir up some excitement."

"I bet you do," she says. She turns and heads through the glass doors, down the stairs. Still he follows.

"What it is," he's saying, "is usually I show up somewhere, and then things start happening from there." He's talking faster now, as if he knows he's running out of time. "Still," he says, "I'm what you'd call a principled person."

"Principled," she says.

"Thing is," he says, "sad fact is, you tell someone that and it makes them suspect you even more."

"True," she says, pushing open the door to the platform. She is relieved other people are waiting, standing there, potential witnesses.

"I'm a pretty vulnerable person," he says.

"Now it's you who's got me mixed up with someone else," she says. Surrounded by others, she feels more able to cross him. "Soon as someone starts telling me what kind of person they are, then I know they're trouble."

"Now, Ruth," he says. "I'm just keeping you company here, while you're waiting. We don't even have to talk, you know."

A cluster of pigeons settles close, and he stamps his feet, scattering them. Ruth stares down at the space between the rails—cigarette butts, plastic forks and knives, discarded baggage tags.

"I really grow on people," he says. "Maybe you don't think you'll like me more than you do right now, but don't worry, you will."

"I trust my first impressions," she says, not meaning to break her silence. "I'm a good judge of character."

"Then I got nothing to worry about." Scott claps his hands together. When he speaks again, his voice is softer, almost as if he's speaking to himself. "Hot morning like this," he says, "you just know it's going to wear you out. Sometimes, at the end of the day your body's tired, you know, and your head is heavy, and all you want is to hold onto someone."

"That's my train," Ruth says.

It arrives with a hiss, its doors sliding open. Ruth steps in and listens as the door slides closed behind her. Scott still watches her, still stands on the platform. Ruth almost can not believe it, the fact of having something solid between them. She sits on the far side of the train, exhausted, as it begins moving; she lets the familiarity of the passing scene calm her.

The train is half empty. People rest suitcases in the aisle, while others wear uniforms that are some variation of her own. The window next to her head is etched with initials and foul words, taunts and threats. Through it, she glimpses the stones of the graveyard, flashing white, and then they are gone and the bushes thicken into tangled sumac and vines. Shopping carts glint, taken down and grown over. The river runs close by on the other side of the train, then veers away, then is gone. On the right, dingy walls rise up; wherever the vines have been pulled down, spray paint shows. The train passes the junkyards of Grays Ferry, passes white tanks full of unknown poison, pipes snaking every which way from their rounded tops.

A car lies abandoned on the slope, half buried and all rust, without windows, the doors and trunk sprung open as if waiting. Just beyond it, on a bridge trestle, is Terrell's gift to Ruth—in red and orange spray paint, tall letters say HAPPY BIRTHDAY RUTH. Below it, in blue, is the figure of a man with his arms outstretched, his penis hanging down around his ankles. Of course, Terrell denied he'd done the second part, and she could hardly punish him for surprising her like that.

Ruth laughs to herself, watching the naked blue man slide past, and then she thinks of Scott, and she wonders if it is true that he knows

67

Terrell or if he was only using Terrell's name, making it all up. If she asked Terrell, he might not give her a straight answer; he'll tell her anything, sometimes, just to provoke her.

The train rises above a little power station, clusters of transformers. It only takes twenty minutes, this ride, and she knows it by heart. Last there are the hotels and motels, and then the airport itself. She waits for terminal D, and steps off into the roar of planes as they climb and land, a sound like a giant piece of paper being slowly torn.

The air is cool inside the terminal. She climbs the stairs, avoiding escalators; she'll be standing still for the next eight hours. Taking the card from her pocket, she hangs it on its chain around her neck. It says who she is, with a tiny picture to compare to her face, a colored stripe which says what level of clearance she has. She dodges a floor buffer, then a team of janitors.

"You're never late," Dwayne says, standing behind the United counter.

"I see you're back," she says.

"Scenic Bermuda," he says, drawing out the syllables. "Sandy beaches, clear skies. You could have been there." He winks, and the gold stud in his nose flashes. Dwayne takes advantage of all the free travel available to him, and he is always trying to talk Ruth into coming along. They have a variation of this conversation every week or so.

"Tell me you're not tempted." Dwayne's beard is shaved thin along his jawline, an attempt to make his chin look firmer than it actually is; the hair on his head is the same length as his beard, making the whole thing look, to Ruth, like some kind of helmet.

"Florida's next," he's saying. "Either that or the D.R. Think about it, now, sister."

"I'm thinking," she says, still moving, heading down the terminal, toward the security station.

José waves when he sees her coming. He takes his jacket from the back of his chair, then walks out the way she's come.

Neighborhood

"Get some sleep," Ruth says, taking up her position. She settles into the hum of fluorescent lights, the music constant yet so faint it is almost subliminal. She has to concentrate to notice it as she readies herself for the parade of bored white people, all about to step into metal cylinders and allow themselves to be hurtled above the earth. Usually, she works the night shift; every fourth week is an exception.

The conveyor belt leads into the scanner, and Ruth controls its speed with a foot pedal; she stops it when she wants a longer look at something. Black rubber strips hang down from the scanner's mouth, a veil that keeps the X rays inside. A wall of glass separates the incoming and outgoing passengers, and it is only opaque behind Ruth, so no one else can see what she does, the images on her screen.

The hours go quickly when things are busy. She gazes through the tissuelike ghosts of bags, straight to the hard shapes of keys, lipsticks, change purses like one more membrane, coins round and dark, hair brushes like strange weapons, condoms just strings of black O's. She never tires of it—both deciphering the shapes on the screen and the simple pleasures of seeing the private things of strangers. Sometimes, as they approach, she tries to guess what they are carrying; she is often surprised. Once she believed a businessman had a snake coiled in his briefcase, and it turned out to be an eight-foot-long braided whip. Once a Halloween mask stared back at her from the screen, dark and horned with white, empty eyes. Twice she'd found handguns, and both times the people acted shocked, as if they'd merely forgotten to take them out, as if carrying a pistol in your briefcase was a normal thing to do, most days. Another time, two boys worked as a team—one went through the metal detector and waited there, as if he had baggage coming; when a wealthy-looking person put luggage on the belt, the boy's accomplice would push in front of the person; the accomplice's pockets would be full of coins, steel toes in his shoes; while he set off the metal detector, the first boy got away with the bag.

Ruth watches it all. Her alertness rises with the level of traffic.

69

When it slows, though, she walks over to the tall windows and looks over the tarmac, at all the baggage trailers, the planes parked at the gates with their tails in the air. At the end of this day she'll take the train back home, drink one beer, then lie awake and wonder when Terrell will return. She sometimes almost fantasizes that something will happen to him, that her worrying will become true. Without him, her life would be simple; perhaps too simple, though she knows something will always rise to fill and tangle.

Carts honk and swing around her, loaded down with the aged and confused. Ruth looks out over the satellite dishes and aerials that cover the tower where air traffic controllers keep watch for crashes, over all the planes loaded to fly to distant places, to return with other people in place of those taken away. She has no fear of flying, but she has no desire to get away, nor to sleep in a bed someone else has made for her, nor to walk on white beaches while acting as if she's escaped something. Like Dwayne, she has free travel vouchers—she works for the airline, not the airport—yet she never uses them. The reason she turns Dwayne down, whenever he asks her out, is that she needs a person who can stay in a place, who can handle that and understand it. She wants a man to sit in her kitchen—the ceiling plaster buckling overhead, the wallpaper smelling of greens cooking down—and laugh and talk to her.

When Ruth turns, she sees a flash of blue, the back of a figure as it slips between others, disappearing into a crowd. She remembers the man, Scott; the familiarity of her job has almost helped her forget him. If it is him, if he comes back, she'll call security. She'll make up a story, if she has to, and they'll believe her. Now she watches a briefcase pass through. Papers, a calculator, a cell phone. Simple. Then another lull sets in.

It's as if he'd looked straight through the walls of her house and seen her inside, known what to say to get her going. She wonders what it would mean to pump a house full of concrete and whether, once all

Neighborhood

the siding had bent and rusted away, all the wood rotted to nothing, if there would be concrete ghosts left behind, like thickened air, a reminder of the space where someone had once lived and which now had no inside. She imagines the textures on the concrete, the back of framed pictures, pieces of metal chairs, and other things floated to the surface, almost recognizable. She cannot forget what Scott said, just as she boarded the train, about someone to hold onto at the end of the day.

Nine
Magnetism

S cott and Ray rest side by side in the engine house. Neither one can sleep. Ray lights a cigarette and the walls flicker, pale for a moment; then it's dark again.

"You getting any closer," he says, "with that woman you're after?"

"Could be," Scott says. "It's real slow and steady, you know. She's coming around, but it's real gradual."

"Right. And what about the other one?"

"What one's that?"

"The last one," Ray says. "The one who robbed the place with you. How'd you lose hold of her?"

Scott rolls onto his side, thinking, listening to the trucks on the highway. He doesn't exactly want to tell the story, yet he also wants Ray to hear it, to know these things.

"There's lots of stories," he says. "How we met, some of the things we did. All the traveling. But that's not the sad part. That's not where I learned anything. Chrissie—did I tell you her name was Chrissie? We were hitchhiking together, middle of last winter. Up along North Dakota, into Montana."

"And whose baby was it?" Ray says.

They are whispering, but still their voices echo.

"Chrissie's," Scott says. "Man, you got some memory."

"I mean, who was the father?"

"She never said. It doesn't matter. She was pregnant before I ever met her, you know, and she was really close. I was thinking about it all the time. What we'd do. And then those lottery tickets were blank and everything."

"You didn't tell me that, before."

"They were useless," Scott says. "Not one bit lucky."

"Tell it all," Ray says.

"Well, I wanted to help her, you know. I had this idea. This'll sound stupid. Thing is, we weren't together, exactly—she didn't let me touch her like that. I was just trying to see ahead."

"So what was the idea?"

"I never told her. I just had this vision of us, after the baby came, out there in a western town. And we'd be living in a house painted all a pale blue, and I'd be looking after them out there. I wanted to take responsibility. I wanted to be responsible, there." He shifts, his shoulder against Ray's; neither pulls away.

"Chrissie went into labor in Big Timber. That's in Montana. We got to the hospital, the clinic, in time. Everything went all right. It took hours, all night, but it went smooth, they said. I was out in the hallway, going outside to smoke, standing in a blizzard, beyond wired, waiting.

"The next day, I saw him. The baby. Through the window, you know; they didn't let me hold him. He was beautiful, beyond beautiful. Healthy, they told me, and so was Chrissie. Thing was, they wouldn't let me visit her. Said I wasn't her husband, wasn't the baby's father. There was something else behind it, though—I could tell. I waited two

73

days, sleeping there, walking through the snow to the gas station for some food. I was hoping she could see me through a window, that she'd ask for me when I got back."

"Tell it," Ray says, filling the silence when Scott pauses.

"On the third day, a nurse lent me a twenty. She said to get a decent meal. I went across the street, just across the street to a diner there. I could watch the clinic through the big window, and I sat there, after I finished eating. It was warm, and I smoked cigarette after cigarette, thinking ahead, about the blue house and all that. After a while I realized a taxi was parked in front of the clinic, idling, smoke jerking out from its tailpipe.

"A nurse, the same nurse, came out of the clinic, pushing a wheelchair with someone in it. When the person stood up, I saw it was Chrissie. And she held the baby, all wrapped in blankets. She bent down, climbed into the taxi, and it drove away."

Scott stops talking. His eyes are on Ray, but all he can make out is the silhouette of the old man's face.

"You quit smoking," Ray said.

"That's for the tests," Scott says. "And everything."

"You didn't do anything wrong," Ray says.

"I didn't do something right. I never saw her again."

"Unlucky," Ray says.

"No."

"You think you've been lucky?"

"Lucky or unlucky doesn't matter," Scott says, "looking back. I wanted to be responsible, you know? When things haven't worked out, that's when I didn't do it right, when I didn't try hard enough."

Ray doesn't argue. Scott listens to his friend's breathing, and he realizes that telling the story did not hurt, as he'd feared it would. He feels right to have told Ray, honest; he has shared a secret, which is what friends do. He matches his breathing with Ray's. Gradually, he joins him in sleep.

Magnetism

When Scott awakens in the darkness, hours later, he realizes the old man's arms are wrapped around him, holding him; his own arms are grasping back. Ray is asleep. Scott extricates himself, lying there, and when the old man sleepily reaches out again, he does not resist.

The second time Scott awakens, he opens his eyes and stares across the floor. Light filters in through the dirty skylights in the roof and the high windows, which aren't boarded up. A cockroach—on its back, seemingly dead—suddenly rouses itself, scuttling away. Breathing in, Scott smells fish. The river. Ray is pressed up against him, and there's warmth along the length of where their bodies touch.

Now he hears a sound like hands clapping together, and he knows it's the wings of crows and pigeons outside, lifting off. Something has disturbed them. Next, he hears a car engine draw near, rattling down; after a moment, there are footsteps.

Scott stands, his boots in one hand, his backpack in the other. Slipping outside, he smooths his hair, rubs at his eyes, tucks in his shirt. His boots are stiff and cool. He steps around the corner and sees the man, facing away from him. His immediate thought is to turn and run, but then he thinks of Ray.

"Hey there!" Scott shouts. "Good morning."

The man turns. He is tall and thickly set, perhaps twice the size of Scott. He wears a yellow hard hat, a plaid shirt, a cellular phone on his belt.

"Morning." He gestures with a steaming thermos. Over his shoulder, up the river, crew teams are already rowing, the sun beginning to rise.

Scott stands at the corner of the building, facing the man at the same time as he keeps an eye on the engine house door.

"Walk along here every morning," Scott says. He's talking loudly, hoping to rouse Ray. "Work over at the hospital. Sometimes I stop and look at the buildings here, but I don't touch anything. Gate's broken."

"Plan to reclaim this," the man says. "Reclamation project. Big

75

building's going to be a restaurant. I just came out here to make some initial estimates, you know. Structural appraisals."

"Hundred years ago this was all working," Scott says. "All the city's water, and everything—after that there was the aquarium, I guess, and then the swimming pool."

"And now who knows what kind of activity happens around here," the man says.

"I hear you," Scott says, and then, in the corner of his eye, he sees movement. It's the front wheel of Ray's bike, coming out the door. Stepping sideways, trying to slow the man, Scott keeps talking. "All that grass there was under water," he says, "and water got passed through the engine house, pumped into pools up toward the museum, which wasn't even there, of course."

"You seem to know quite a bit about it," the man says. "Could come out here and give the tours on the weekend."

"Too busy," Scott says. He swivels on his heels, turning the corner with the man. There's no sign of Ray. "Better get to it." Scott heads toward the gate.

"It's all under control," the man says, behind him.

Scott walks past the dried-out fountain, under the overpass. This is the safest time of the day, when the dealers are gone, wherever they go to get their only sleep of the day. There are no men under the trees, and there are never any women here—only the occasional college girl in running shorts, moving too fast to catch, screaming if anyone looks her way. Homeless women stay away, and those who do come around don't last; for them it is safer in the shelters.

A train sits motionless on the tracks, as if resting, deserted. Dipping a rag in the river, he scrubs the front and arms of his jacket as he walks down the gravel of the bank. He slides his pack around and takes out half a bagel from the day before, a jar of baby food. Whipped yams. He's heard people say insanity leads to homelessness, but he knows it's the other way around—the lack of sleep, the poor nutrition, the worrying—

all that drives people beyond. He watches himself. Slugging water from a glass jar, he swallows a handful of vitamins. If today's test goes well, he'll treat himself to the pancake special at IHOP.

Little birds perch in the bushes, twitching their tails, ratcheting their necks as if mechanized. Farther down, where the bushes are taller and thicker, the boy hustlers hang out; sometimes they'll drop their waistbands to show their bare asses as he goes by, and other times they'll stand with their pants torn open, straight up the back seam. It's quiet today. A man's white face flashes once from the foliage, then is gone.

Scott cuts across the tracks, through a half-empty parking lot, and angles toward Market Street. He's not so hungry now, and the night is far in the future. His confidence rises with every step.

At the bank, he checks his hair in the plate-glass window. His face seems fairly clean.

When they unlock the door, he is the first one inside. Vacuum marks show on the carpet. Computers hum. He has almost three thousand dollars now, and he trusts the bank with it because it's clear they have so much more. Standing between the velvet ropes, he waits to be called, his account number memorized. Video cameras point down, and he feels everyone watching him, the people he can see and others hidden in rooms, where he's shown on television screens. He smiles.

The teller waves him over. She has a tattoo of a scissors and comb, crossed, on her forearm.

"Hey, smiley," she says. "Yes, we still have the machine that counts coins."

"That was last week," he says. "I won't be needing that today."

He withdraws five dollars, pockets a handful of free lollipops, asks to use the rest room.

"I'll be in here making some more deposits in the near future," he says. "You can count on that."

The rest room shines. He has to move fast; first he relieves himself, jamming a handful of toilet paper into his pack, stocking up. He takes out his toothbrush and razor, exiting the stall, then runs the water, letting it get hot as he brushes his teeth. He always says he's the kind of person who doesn't get very dirty, but one of his secrets is how much he can accomplish with a sponge. He scrubs between his legs, under his arms, the back of his neck.

His beard grows better on one side than the other. He could have one sideburn, if he wanted it. His whiskers are darker than his hair, and this reminds him of Kenny Rogers; Kenny's beard was perfectly manicured, always the exact same color as his hair—caught between gray and white.

He's half done shaving when a man wearing a suit comes in. He uses the urinal, then washes his hands at the other sink, his shoulder almost touching Scott's. In the mirror, he pretends to look at himself, but he's actually surveying the situation.

"You never locked yourself out of your house?" Scott says.

The man does not reply.

"I have an account here," Scott says to the closing door.

Time is running out. He rinses his face in cold water, cut whiskers circling to the drain. A few nicks under the chin, that's it. Stepping back from the mirror, he smiles. Not bad at all.

Outside, the skin of his face feels red and raw, clean. The heat is coming onto the city. He wants to reach the hospital before he really starts sweating, and it's a fine line, trying to rush without getting overheated. Sticks of lollipops poke him through his pocket; he'll probably give them away, since he avoids sugar when he can. For energy, though, they'll be a decent last resort.

He walks toward the bridge, the river. In the distance, approaching, he sees a man on a bicycle. It's not Ray, though that's not clear at first; it's another old black man, a squeegee like a lance over the handlebars, a bucket hung off the other side.

The train station looms to his right as he crosses the river; seeing it, he thinks of the train heading to the airport, and of Ruth. He's watched her through the singed curtains of the abandoned house, often seen her going to work, and on Sundays, all dressed up, her whole body loose inside a flowered dress, her dark feet strapped by white sandals. The thought quickens his stride. He doesn't want Ruth to forget who he is, yet he doesn't want to approach her near her house again, to frighten her—at least not so much that she'll get someone else involved. He has to be patient. He'd like to take the train to the airport right now, to see her, but he has no time.

At the hospital, everyone wears white. Everything is in motion, and it all seems so clean. The water in the drinking fountain is warm. Scott calls the number on the card they'd given him, using the phone in the lobby. A man's voice says someone will be right down.

Scott waits. He feels no different than those around him, and he's certainly better off than some. They have no idea who he is, whether he's visiting a friend or is a patient himself. This is different than at the drug companies, where he had to wear a different-colored scrub shirt, depending on his trial, and a name tag at all times. Twenty-five dollars it cost, if he was late, which he never was. Here it is different; he'll take less money, every time, to be treated like a human being.

It's Lisa Roberts who comes to the lobby. She points and leads him down the hall, to the elevators.

"Remember me?" he says.

"It's all set up down there," she says, stepping into the elevator. "You just follow their instructions." She's checking her watch; her ankles flex like her feet want to be walking.

"I'm the one," he says. "All those questions. Maybe I've changed a little."

"I don't know if they told you this," she says, "but you'll get a copy of the image from the scan, along with your payment." She just watches the numbers count down, above their heads. Scott realizes they're going underground. The doors open.

"This way," she says; then, "This is Beverly."

Beverly is a short, black woman, matching his smile. Her finger-nails are dark red, long, and curved. She wears a long white coat that hides the shape of her body, her name embroidered over the pocket.

Scott looks around, and the elevator doors are closing. Lisa Roberts is gone.

"How far down you reckon we are?" he says.

"Time is precious," Beverly says.

"I'm with you, there."

Taking his pack from him, she swings it into a locker. The only words he can read on her clipboard are his name.

"I have the key," she says. "Trust me. You wearing any metal? Any metal in your pockets?"

"That safe in there?" he says.

"That's what I said."

"No metal at all," he says.

"Stand here," she says. "Now read the letters on the wall."

"Can't quite make it out."

"Try on these glasses. That better?"

The eyeglasses are all plastic, with square, black frames. Where there had been metal screws, at the temples, there are loops of clear fishing line.

"A little," he says.

"How about these?" She holds out another pair.

"Yes," he says. Everything is suddenly crisp here, underground. Shimmering.

"You're nearsighted, that's all. Follow me." Her white clogs make no sound on the floor. He has to hurry to keep up. Doctor's names are called out over the intercom, code words and numbers for disasters he can only guess at.

The door of the room has a special handle, gaskets like those on a refrigerator. A sign shows a picture of a floor buffer, circled with a slash through it. It reads WARNING: STRONG MAGNETIC FIELD.

Magnetism

Inside, a huge silver torpedo rests on the floor, ten feet high with a hole at one end, tubes sticking out the top. A table stretches from the open end; Beverly gestures that he should sit on it.

"Looks like science fiction," he says. "Hardly seems real." He does not want her to see that he's nervous.

"Just a big magnet," she says. "Simple. You like this, maybe you can move on to the internal cameras, see how you like that."

"You'll probably get some surprises," he says, "when you look at my brain."

"The first test," she says. "You'll hold this handset, here, and hit the right button if the person's expression is happy, left if it's sad, and the middle one if it's neutral. The images will be projected out here; you'll watch them through a little mirror."

"You staying in here?" Scott is on his back now. Beverly is packing pillows around his head, so he can't move it.

"I'll be right behind that window, there."

"I can't see through there."

"I can see you," she says. "The second test is just memory. You'll see. And, whatever you do, don't move."

He feels her take off his boots. He knows his socks are stiff and gray. Next, she lays a thin blanket over him.

"For the noise," she says, her face close again. He feels her fingernails inside his ears, then the foam earplugs, expanding; he can hear nothing but his own breathing, the sounds of his body.

Beverly closes down something like a plastic birdcage, around his head, close to his face. The table begins to slide, feeding him to the machine. A mirror is attached inside the cage, tilted above his eyes. In it, past his feet, he sees Beverly walking away, returning with a screen, and then leaving him alone again, closing the door behind her.

He can hardly move his arms, it is so tight. He does not know if he can stand it; only embarrassment keeps him from calling out, trying to extricate himself. He thinks of all the stories he was told as a boy, about

81

being buried alive, and he tries to breathe, to calm himself, to think of something else; he wonders about the internal cameras Beverly mentioned, how it would be with a cable down his throat, to see his heart at work, all that space in there.

Despite the earplugs, he hears a plinking sound, a plunking, and then another, like a ratchet tightening around his head. He hears them and feels them at the same time, though it is not painful. It rises to a jackhammer, then eases off; the plinking and plunking resumes.

The light changes, and then the faces start shifting past him. Happy, sad, neutral. They are mostly old people, in black-and-white, staring down the tube into his mirror. Too many of them have half-assed smiles, tending toward grimaces, though he knows that his own smile, even when he forces it, makes him feel better. He does not want to get anything wrong, and his fingers are sweaty on the handset, the noises all around him. The people look out as if they live in some other world, where all they do is simulate expressions and never have actual emotions. They exaggerate to make it easy for him, to show they understand.

Inside the machine, he has the sensation of motion, travel. He thinks about cars, his plans for the future, and he wonders about how thoughts lead to actions and how actions lead to thoughts. He imagines Ray's garden, all that work for beauty, and he thinks of Ray holding onto him last night, while the black river ran past outside the engine house, the darkness and the moon. It was the soundest sleep he can remember.

"Scott!" It's Beverly's voice, right next to his head, as if she is inside the machine, lying alongside him. "Don't fall asleep," she says.

"No chance of that," he says. He cannot hear his voice.

"Next test, I'll show you some faces again; hit the right button if they were in that first group, if you've seen them before, and the left one if you haven't."

"You didn't warn me," he says.

"Exactly," she says, but when the images come it's easier than he expected, as if his brain had been picking up details—sizes of ears, tilts of heads, strange wrinkles, twisted lips—while he'd hardly been paying attention. He goes through the whole series and, after a pause, the lights come on. In the mirror, he sees Beverly, walking toward him. He begins to slide back out of the machine.

She takes off the birdcage, then the earplugs from his ears. She's moving as quickly and silently as before, wheeling the screen out of the way, stacking pillows. Scott sits up, swings his legs over the side of the table, above his boots. He's a little surprised to find himself in the same room, and he looks around for a clock, wondering what kind of time has passed. Half bewildered, he eases himself down from the table, reaches for his boots.

"That's it?" he says, clapping his hands.

"Yes," she says.

"You were probably a little amazed," he says, "when you saw my brain working."

"It'll be a while before we know how the scan went," she says. "Whether you moved or anything."

Scott just smiles. He takes off the glasses and the edges of the room retreat from him. He has no idea where he is; somewhere down in the ground, under the hospital. The nearest people to them could be miles away. He watches Beverly; she does not really remind him of Ruth, except that she is black and a woman. That is enough to get him thinking.

"Listen," he says. "Hyperthetical question—how do you think a guy like me could get someone like you to spend some time with him?"

"Let's pretend you didn't ask me that question," Beverly says. "It's not going to happen." She stands in the door, the key in her hand, motioning for him to follow.

He looks back once, at the machine he was inside, then hurries after her. She holds out his backpack, and he takes it. The sound of the elevator door startles him; it opens right next to him.

"Can you go up by yourself?" she says, as if she doesn't want to be in the elevator alone with him. "First floor, then follow the signs out onto the street."

"I can," he says, and as he turns away he slips the plastic glasses into his pocket. The door closes, and the floor beneath his feet begins to rise.

He hurries down the hallway, between people, stretchers swooping around him. On the street, he feels surrounded by space. The air is hot and heavy, thick in his throat. He is thirsty, hungry. Taking out his glass jar, he drinks from it, water splashing down his throat. He's thinking of pancakes.

When he slips on the eyeglasses, he cannot believe it. Everything is vivid, he feels even more aware; he's always believed his vision was perfect, and now this, almost as if his eyes can catch up to the speed of his mind. He can read signs, and the numbers on license plates. People's faces leap out at him from distances, all the way across the street, and they all remind him of faces from the test. Happy, sad, and neutral, they pass around him. A helicopter circles above, its rotors chopping into visibility, setting itself atop the hospital. A billboard all the way down by the river, over the expressway, reads GET LUCKY.

Ten

Spirals

Terrell comes out of his house, into the morning sun, and sees Scott standing on the corner of Kater and Twenty-fourth—waiting, stepping out onto the street to get a better look at the house. This is not the first time Terrell has seen him there, had to walk past him, across the street; this morning, though, Scott is crossing, to cut him off. He can't be avoided. Terrell shifts direction, heading straight for him. He breathes in, to expand his chest, and holds his arms out from his sides.

"You following me?" he says. "What's your problem?"

"Not exactly. I'm just watching over you a little, Terrell. No problem. Hell, you know me." Scott's still wearing the cowboy boots, the blue jacket, and a striped dress shirt. His eyes are framed by square, cheap-looking plastic glasses.

"So you know my name," Terrell says. "And where I live. So what?"

"I'll just come clean, then," Scott says. He smiles. "Thing of it is,

85

I got an interest in you—you and your sister both. Nothing to be scared of."

"I'm not."

"Good, then we're getting somewhere." Scott steps closer; his shadow falls across Terrell's feet. "What you-all need," he says, "is a man's point of view."

"I'm a man," Terrell says.

Scott laughs, tilting his head back, his hands on his hips. "Getting there," he says. "Maybe. You know, Terrell, back when I was a boy like you, I hurt some people, took some things that didn't belong to me—was a general pain in the ass. And you know what was the worst part of it?"

"White guy looking like you," Terrell says. "Stand here long enough and someone'll mess with you. Sure thing."

"You ever met anyone who's ambidextrous? No one wants to mess with me." Scott takes off the glasses, cleans them on his shirttail.

"That like double-jointed?" Terrell says. "I heard that's a lie—no one's really double-jointed."

"It's more like both-handed," Scott says, "and it's no lie." He puts the glasses back on, his hands in his pockets. "And it's the hemispheres—you know that word?—of the brain, one hand to one side and the other to the other."

"What?"

"One side keeps track of everything around you and the other thinks about it, you know. But with me it happens all at the same time. Not one, then the other."

"You wish."

"Anyway," Scott says, "the worst part about everything I did was that I got away with it. Every single time. I didn't have to learn. Listen to me—you got two big decisions in your life, that's all. One, what you're going to do, and two, who you're going to do it with. You see the woman for you, you can't let anything get in your way."

86

Spirals

"I never saw you with a woman," Terrell says. "Only seen you hanging out with that old bicycle man. Or maybe you like boys, the way you been waiting around for me."

"Don't you worry about me," Scott says. "The main thing is, once you decide what you want to do, you got to stick to it. That's the main thing. You got to get a grip on things. You don't ever want to get in a situation where go equals whoa and whoa equals go, you know what I mean?"

"No," Terrell says.

"See?" Scott says. "Exactly what I'm saying."

Gasoline rainbows are congealed in the dirty puddle by Scott's feet. The leather of his cowboy boots is worn down and thin; the shapes of his five toes are visible, pushing against it. His yellow-and-brown shirt seems familiar to Terrell, as if it's one of his father's shirts, the ones he didn't want—Ruth told him this, when cleaned out the closet, donated the shirts to the Salvation Army. Terrell listens to what Scott's saying, and it sounds like pure bullshit, especially the way he says it; still, he almost wants to believe some of it. He likes to listen.

"You see," Scott says, "I'm optimistic, not desperate. That's why you didn't walk past me, why you didn't walk away. I'm interested in you. Aren't you interested in me?"

"You're just trying to get something."

"Maybe so," Scott says. "But maybe everyone gives as much as they get."

"Remember," Terrell says, "what you told me about having to test your friends?"

"Finding out I was right on that one?"

"I don't know."

"Got you thinking now, don't I?"

"About where I'm supposed to be," Terrell says. He's thinking about Swan, Darnay, John. He turns away and begins walking up Twenty-fourth.

"No matter what," Scott's saying, behind him, "no matter who you are, everyone can use a little help. See you later, now. Chances are you'll be seeing plenty of me."

Terrell's late. He doesn't know what time it is, since he only heard it on the radio in the kitchen, and that was before he started talking to Scott. He looks back, but Scott is not following; he just stands there, skinny and pathetic, looking up the street, swaying as if there's music in his head.

Terrell crosses South Street, past old people in bathing suits, waiting outside the gate to the public pool. Their skin sags, towels wrapped around their waists, caps with rubber petals on their heads. Row houses in this neighborhood are fixed up, with colored plates and dried flowers in the windows, the stickers and signs of burglar alarm companies, brass names and numbers pounded into doors. Taxis bounce and swerve through potholes. Terrell looks back once more; Scott is gone.

He arrives at the same time as Darnay. John and Swan are waiting. The four boys slide their palms together, then step back to look each other over, to let things settle.

"That's one ugly shirt, Darnay," Swan says. He's holding a dirty coil of clothesline in one hand. His cheek is swollen, but no one mentions it.

"You don't know anything," Darnay says. His shirt is dark brown, too big, a gold UPS patch over the pocket. "Only way you can wear this stuff is if it's stolen. That's how it is. Are we ready or what?"

This is John's neighborhood. In some places the roots of trees have lifted the slabs of sidewalk, so it's all uneven; down by John's house, the sidewalk's been replaced by red brick.

"My mom has aerobics," John says. "Right at ten o'clock." His T-shirt says HOMEBOY across the front.

"Here she comes," Terrell says, and they all retreat into the alley, flatten themselves against the fence. Staring straight ahead with both hands on the wheel, her red hair pulled back, John's mother accelerates past. The station wagon shines.

"All right," Darnay says.

"Let's wait a second," Terrell says. "In case she forgot something."

"She does, sometimes," John says.

They wait. Across the street, the fountain splashes in Fitler Square, between the statue of the goat and the one of the bear. Some kids are playing on the brass tortoises.

"That's long enough," Swan says.

They walk past John's house without looking at it, then go around the side, down the driveway, under the basketball hoop. From behind the tall fence, the dog begins barking.

"Lady," John says. "Easy, girl."

"Lady?" Swan says. "This is going to be even better than I thought."

"Quiet," Darnay says. He swings the gate open and the dog slips out, not sure which one to go to first, whining, wagging her tail so hard her whole body goes from side to side. She snuffles at their feet, licks at their hands. She's a golden retriever, tan feathers of hair on the backs of her legs, on her ears, a dopey look on her face. Swan ties the clothesline to her collar and hands the other end to John.

"Leave the latch open," Darnay says. "That's important."

"No, close it," Terrell says. "That way it doesn't seem like she could've gotten out by herself."

They head back out toward the street. A striped cat slides under a fence and runs silently beneath a car; the dog doesn't see it. A little farther, an old woman, coming from the other direction, smiles at the sight of the boys.

"You know her?" Darnay says.

"No," John says.

"You crying?" Darnay says.

"I'm not," John says, even though they can see the tears on his face.

"Man, what do you think we're going to make you do, kill her or something?"

"I don't know," John says.

"We could anchor her down with something," Darnay says. "See how she swims. Man, I'm just kidding you. Maybe."

The three of them had come up with John's test, but now Darnay's taking over the specifics. They pass down through the empty playground, through a hole in the fence, across the tracks, right to the edge of the river, where they take a left and keep walking. A white plastic bag parachutes from the South Street Bridge, lands in the Schuylkill, and jerks along downstream; it stays on the surface, as if the water is solid. Dark wedges of clouds slide across the sky, hardly reflecting in the river.

"If we were going to kill her," Darnay says. "I'd just take this here and do it myself. Pow."

Everyone stares at the gun, the pistol in his hand, pointed straight at Lady. No one says a thing. The dog pants, wags her tail. They stand still for a moment.

"So we're not going to kill her?" John says.

"Afraid to lose your dog?" Terrell says.

"You might get her back," Darnay says. "You might not."

"Where'd you get the gun?" Swan says.

"Just got it. That's all."

"Can we shoot it?" Terrell says.

"I'll think about it. Only have a couple bullets, and they cost money." Darnay puts the gun back inside his pants, the UPS shirt flapping over to cover it.

They keep walking, just the same, though now everything feels different. The dog prances along ahead of them, sniffing the ground. Dry dirt kicks up, and Terrell tries to step where it's packed down, to save the whiteness of his shoes.

Spirals

"How long you had her?" Darnay says. The *D* shaved into the back of his head is hard to see now, mostly grown in.

"I was five," John says. "We got her for me."

"You love your little dog?" Swan says.

"No," John says, glancing at Darnay's face for approval or some reaction. Darnay's looking over at the beer distributor's warehouse, its curved metal roof shining in the sun. They pass it, heading south into Grays Ferry, past junkyards and vacant lots.

"Hey, Swan," Darnay says. "Saw your girlfriend the other day. Lakeesha. Wearing jeans with a zipper that went all the way around the crotch, you know, so they could be zipped right in two."

"Saw her with her friends," John says. "They all had baby pacifiers in their mouths. What up with that?"

"Jealous," Swan says. "That's all you are." He's hanging back from them, walking next to Terrell.

"You seen her since that day?" Terrell says.

Swan takes an empty beer bottle by the neck and throws it, end over end, into the river. His 'Sixers shorts are pulled low, hiding his knees. His jaw is working, his mouth closed. When he speaks, only Terrell can hear.

"I can't stop thinking about it."

"Did you like it?"

"I don't know yet."

Lady looks back at them, every few minutes, and continues to lead. Off to the left, the power plant rises with all its wires and transformers, its smokestack coughing away. Fences circle it, topped with razor wire. The bushes along the river look tired, leaning against each other.

"It must feel good," Terrell says, "to have your test done, anyway, and everything."

"That's not it," Swan says. "It's the girl."

"Don't get hung up on her," Terrell says, repeating what he's heard people say. "She might do it with you again, maybe she won't—there's lots of them out there, you know what I'm saying?"

"It just seemed kind of backward. I never even talked to her or anything like that."

"So talk to her."

"I want you to talk to her, first, for me."

"What?" Terrell says. "Why?"

"It's easier for you—you're not involved in the same way. Just tell her I want to see her. That's all. See what she says."

"I'll think about it," Terrell says.

"You two walk around like boyfriend and girlfriend," Darnay says, looking back. "Only I'm not sure who's the boy. Catch up, here; this is far enough. Maybe we'll go further once we're done with this part."

"What part?"

At first it seems that he's taken out the gun again, but it's a battery-powered clipper in his hand. He flips the switch and the blades vibrate, their edges gone blurry. He kneels down.

"John," he says. "You hold her. She bites anyone, it should be you." Darnay looks up at Terrell and Swan. "You two have to take over if my hand gets tired."

"Seems like we're doing too much of the work," Swan says, "for this to count as John's test."

"It'll count," Darnay says. " 'Cause his dad is proud of the dog, and his mom loves her, right?"

John doesn't answer, but he's no longer crying.

"This dog won't ever trust him again," Darnay says. "And John gets to do the hard part all by himself, watching it all and knowing he did it, and he'll have to make LOST DOG signs, even, hang them all over the telephone poles and everything."

"But we don't get to watch that part," Swan says.

"John," Darnay says. "You happy?"

"Yes," John says. "No."

"Hold the damn dog."

The first cut goes straight along Lady's spine. She shivers. Darnay has to pull her tail out straight because it's down between her legs. Fur collects in the blades; he shakes out the clumps.

"My mom won't even notice I used them," he says. "This isn't going to take long at all."

Lady strains away, but John holds her tight. Darnay takes the hair right off her flat skull and her eyes are closed, wincing. Terrell slaps at a fly on the back of his neck. He's enjoying this, trying to imagine what will happen next—how John will explain it, if he has to, and just what is going through his pasty head now. Terrell wonders when they all began to turn so mean, and at the same time he's glad they have. It feels like a necessary change.

A car rattles across the bridge above, unseen. Lady's fur blows along the ground, collecting in a straight line against the vegetation at the path's edge. There's no one around. No one else watching. Lady sneezes, then sneezes again. She's starting to look like some kind of pig or goat, hanging from a hook in a window at the Italian Market.

"Clippers are getting hot," Darnay says. "She doesn't like that."

"Watch out for her tits," Terrell says.

Darnay straightens up, brushing fur from his knee. He switches the clippers off.

"Terrell," he says. "You know, I saw you this morning, with that guy." He looks at Swan, then down at John, who's still holding the dog. "Same white guy we saw in the woods, the other day, and there's Terrell, talking to him. Sure the two of you don't have something going on?"

"He asked me for a quarter," Terrell says. "So what?"

"Two of them looked pretty tight—man had his arm around your shoulder, whispering to you."

"He never touched me," Terrell says.

"Man," Darnay says, "that's not my business. But this is how it is,

93

where some of us have got tested—like Swan, we can trust him—but you, we can't tell if you're lying or what."

"I'm not lying," Terrell says.

"Maybe," Darnay says.

Terrell reaches out and pushes Darnay's shoulder. Darnay just sets the razor on the ground. His face is calm, his lips not pulled into a snarl. John and Swan back away, silently, knowing they don't have to pick a side.

"No way," Terrell says. "I'm not fighting anyone holding a gun."

Darnay takes out the pistol, turns, and hands it to Swan. He comes back with both arms in front of him, to push Terrell's chest, to start the fight, and Terrell slaps them away and hits Darnay in the side of the head, a glancing blow, trying to get in fast. He punches Darnay in the ribs, solid, then backs out, his hands up. He feels the heat run along his skin, his scalp tight and his shoulders clenching. In his ears he feels the rush of his heart, he hears the dog barking.

"Oh, yes," Darnay says. He comes straight in with his right hand, swinging all the way around. Terrell ducks it, head-butts him low, and catches a punch in the back, along his spine. Darnay shoves him off balance, then hops sideways and catches him right in the neck. Terrell goes down, tripping over something behind him; he lies on his side, gasping, his windpipe full of hot sand.

It's all happened so quickly, and he's trying to think. He doesn't get up, but it's not that he's hurt—he's confused, wondering why Darnay isn't already on top of him. Terrell's fought him before, and John, even Swan; they've all fought each other, and it's always the same. A few punches, tearing at clothes, and then the kicking, which only starts when someone's stopped worrying about looking cool. That's where the fight really begins; then, once someone's down, the others either break it up or join in.

Darnay turns away, points to the dog, and brushes at his clothes like it's time to get back to business. No one even looks at Terrell, lying there. In a moment, he hears the sound of the clippers. He pulls himself to his feet. He doesn't feel like the fight is over, but the time has passed when he could start it again; he feels no release—usually he feels better after a fight, even when he loses. Now he's not sure how he feels.

Lady has tufts of fur under her tail, around her feet and ears. The backward knees of her hind legs flex, as if they're too thin to hold her. Her snout is ragged, a few whiskers remaining. She looks like a new kind of animal, or one that's gone extinct.

Terrell stands watching. No one looks at him. There's blood in his mouth, where his teeth cut the inside of his cheek. He tries to remember what the fight was about, how it started. He's thinking Darnay probably doesn't even have any bullets for the gun, though he won't say so.

Lady stretches to the end of the rope, wagging the bone of her tail, faintly whining, trying to lick their hands. Terrell pets her, and she feels smooth, then bristly. Tiny red cuts show here and there, and the bones are visible beneath her skin.

"That's one ugly dog of yours," Swan says to John.

"Hold her again," Darnay says. He unties the rope from Lady's collar, and pulls the collar over her head, the tags jangling, her ears pressed forward, then throws it into the river, where it splashes down, all sound lost. Almost immediately, the water's surface is smooth again.

Next, he takes out a Magic Marker and begins writing on the dog. He draws X's and O's, spirals around her eyes. BAD DOG he writes on one side, WHITE NIGGA on the other. She looks like a sad cartoon, bewildered, her tongue hanging out. Darnay draws swirls and lightning bolts, sharp triangles, horns atop her head. On her chest, beneath her snout, he writes PUSSY EATER.

They are all laughing, and Darnay is watching Terrell, catching his eye to be sure everything's all right, to make it clear he wants Terrell to be laughing, too.

95

Then the boys walk farther down the river, along the tracks. Darnay has the rope tied around Lady's neck, now, and she follows reluctantly, her tail between her legs.

Finally, they reach a place beyond where they've ever been, where the ground is dark and smells like oil. Pieces of metal shine weakly, dull in the dead grass. Darnay ties the end of the rope to the door handle of an abandoned car, and the boys walk away, back in the direction they've come. Lady, left behind, watches them go. No matter how loudly she barks, it will be a long time before anyone finds her.

Eleven

Inside Out

Part of what drew Ruth to this job was the rush of people; she loves to be caught in crowds, to feel an old woman press against her, fat men and thin squeezing by, the pressure of shoulders and hips, all straining and struggling to move. Sometimes she makes it harder on them, delaying the separation. In the middle of the night like this, though, there are not enough people; everyone stays as far from each other as they can, each taking as much space as possible. Ruth smiles at the surveillance cameras, she passes businessmen talking on cellular phones, unfolding computers.

She is on her break, walking around the airport's terminals, trying to keep her blood circulating. It's late, but the last rush of red-eye flights is still to come. Announcements echo, pages repeat names three times and then abandon them; bars have been pulled down in front of most of the newsstands and stores—she doesn't need another soft pretzel nor a personal pizza, not even a diet soda. She walks on, picking up her

97

pace. Along the ticket counters, velvet ropes stretch out, ready to herd people into lines, all the spaces between them empty.

"Hey, beautiful," Dwayne says. "Slow down there."

"Break's almost over," she says.

"Always is," he says, shaking a newspaper, folding it in two. "Check this out—says this family's dog got stolen; found it three days later, in a pound in south Philly. Lucky it didn't get put down."

"How do they know it was stolen?" Ruth says. "It could've just run away."

Dwayne waves her closer. The wall behind him is lined with arrival and departure times. The diamond in his nose glints, then goes dull again. As he points to the paper, he spills a cup of baggage tags across the counter. Ruth picks up a few from the floor.

"No one wants to use these things, anyway," he says. "They all think putting their address on one will tip someone off, so they'll know your house or wherever you live is empty. Like a bunch of thieves hang around here, reading people's luggage tags."

"So no one gets robbed," she says, "and they lose their luggage instead."

"Right," he says, then speaks again, quickly, before she can turn away. "Whether the dog was stolen," he says, "that's not the strange thing about the situation. Listen to this—when they found the dog, all its fur was shaved off, and it had writing all over its body. 'Sexually explicit and racially derogatory words, along with strange symbols.' "

"Why would someone do a thing like that?"

"That's the question," Dwayne says. "I just hope it doesn't catch on."

"It's the exact kind of thing," she says. "There a picture?"

"No. Why would you want to see that?"

"Curious," she says, reaching out.

Rather than handing the paper over or turning it toward her, Dwayne steps on the luggage scale and comes around the counter. She senses the bulk of him, the heat of his body next to hers. He spreads out the paper—the article's in the back of the City section—and his hands are thick, his fingers long, his nails perfectly trimmed.

"See," he says, "this detective says they're not ruling out witchcraft, even voodoo, but they got to have an expert look at the symbols."

Ruth reads, feeling him watch her. It surprises her that she isn't repulsed by his proximity; instead, she finds it somehow comforting. She notices a couple of whiskers astray from the careful line of his beard, razor bumps on his throat. She smells the spice of his cologne.

"This is all close to your neighborhood," he says. "Don't you live around there?"

"What do you know about where I live?"

"What do I have to do," he says, trying to laugh it off, "to get you to come out with me sometime?"

"Florida or the Virgin Islands?" she says.

"No reason to joke about it," he says. "Doesn't have to be like that. Could take you to a show, dinner."

"How about lunch?" she says. "You could just come by my place, since you know so much about it. Of course, that'd mean you'd have to stay in town."

"No problem," Dwayne says. "What days are you off?"

"Sunday and Tuesday," she says, beginning to walk away. "Don't pretend you can't find my number."

"I'll call," he says.

"If you come, don't forget your dog."

"I don't have a dog," Dwayne says.

"You're safe, then," she says, heading back to her post.

She doubts Dwayne will show or even call, and she wonders if she could get involved with someone who sees her standing here every day, walking by in this uniform, her face more tired with every hour.

She works alone when it's late like this, though at the push of a button she could have a whole team here. And the security men who decide who will be searched or taken for questioning—based on prior information, criminal profiles—can appear suddenly, as if they are hidden somewhere, always watching. Some days her superiors give her special briefings about guns made entirely of plastic, updates on recent hijackings around the world. She lets them know that her security is always heightened.

A cluster of passengers comes through, and she steps on the pedal for the conveyor belt that pulls their baggage into the scanner. When a passenger sets off the metal detector, she has to walk around and do the wand herself—up each side, between the legs; it's always steel-toed boots or the metal grommets for laces, belt buckles.

The handcuffs are in the last bag in the scanner—dark and round, empty, waiting for wrists. Ruth looks up, to see who they belong to. Her shoulders tighten; her body recognizes him before her mind does.

"New glasses?" she says.

"Kind of. How you been?" When she doesn't answer, Scott points to the frame, the empty doorway of the metal detector. "If a person had a bullet lodged in their body," he says, "from a previous time, would it set this thing off?"

"Hard to say," she says.

He steps through; the detector is silent. He lifts his pack from the metal rollers on the other side of the scanner, and she thinks of the handcuffs. They're not illegal, not exactly.

"That question was hyperthetical," he says, still watching her. He leans forward, then back, his eyes unsteady, his body language a strange combination of hesitance and aggression. "Notice you take the train," he says. "Thinking about buying a car, myself—then I could drive you out here one of these times." He's smiling, accentuating the words by waving his hands in the air. "Or we could just go for a drive, with all the windows rolled down, maybe out into the country or even the beach. Terrell could come. You ever seen the ocean before? I have. Smelled the salt and everything."

Ruth just listens. She wonders why he's talking like this when he's evidently going somewhere—far away, she hopes—but she doesn't ask him. She doesn't want to prolong the conversation.

"Slows down late at night," he says. "Doesn't it?"

"You better get going," she says.

"You're right about that."

Scott can feel her watching him as he walks down the long hall of the terminal, his boot heels echoing. With the glasses, he can see great distances; he can read all the destinations at the gates. Stepping onto a moving walkway, the machine's speed added to his own, he feels almost as if his body could keep up with his mind.

Now Ruth can no longer see him. He steps off the walkway, heads for the rest room. A janitor comes out, holding a mop handle, pushing a bucket on wheels. The tile is gleaming, still drying, all white; the cleanliness of the airport, the way everyone hurries, reminds him of a hospital; only here, everyone is healthy.

He doesn't look at himself in the long mirror, not right away. The sinks are all wet, so he folds down the diapering table and sets his pack there; opening it, he spreads out the things he'll need. He pulls his shirt over his head and quickly sponges himself off. He feels more confident when he's clean—he knows that and wants to get there. Next, he combs his hair back with water, then leans his face close to the mirror. He wonders if his eyelashes are thinner than usual, if they're falling out. Turning, he finds his bottle of vitamins and swallows a few.

He's halfway done shaving when the man comes in. Even shorter than Scott, stocky, he's wearing a tank top that says COUNTRY MUSIC across the front. He begins to comb his hair, then his beard.

"That's my comb," Scott says.

"Sorry," the man says. He sets it down and takes his own comb from his back pocket. "Tired," he says.

The Ambidextrist

"So," Scott says, "Who's your favorite country singer?"

"Randy Travis."

They talk without facing each other, both staring out from the mirror. Scott watches himself having the conversation—shirt off, soap on his face, gesturing with the razor—and it almost slows him.

"Randy Travis," he says, as if he's familiar with Randy Travis. "What do you think of Kenny Rogers?"

"What'd he sing?" the man says. " 'I Love a Rainy Night'? Or was he the 'Footloose' guy?"

"Man." Scott spits in the sink. "That's Kenny Loggins and Eddie Rabbitt you're talking about. I'd hardly call that country music, friend."

"Take it easy, there," the man says.

"It's just, a person would think—what with you wearing that shirt and all—that you'd know what you're talking about."

"Jesus. It's after three in the morning. I don't want any problems."

"Fact is," Scott says, "that you ran into someone who does know what they're talking about."

The man walks out with his hands still wet, the air dryer blowing in his wake. Then it clicks off and Scott is left behind in the silence.

When Ruth sees him returning, she is not exactly surprised. His hair is slicked back, though, and he's wearing a different shirt than before, almost as if he'd flown away somewhere and already returned. She decides not to comment on it, since that is probably what he expects.

"Bet you've been wondering when you'd see me next," he says. His face glows red and smooth.

"I was hoping you'd flown away," she says.

"Not me," he says. "I like to watch the planes take off and land, though. I wouldn't want to be on one, I don't think. Just like to watch and wonder, you know, where those people are off to, in such a hurry."

"That's why you came out here in the middle of the night?"

"No, Ruth. I came to see you."

"And how'd you know I'd be here?"

"I memorized your whole schedule," he says. "Or how did I know you work here?" He taps the side of his head. "It took a little detective work, but that was some time ago. You know, I don't force myself where I'm not wanted. Right now, even, you could tell me to get lost and I would."

"You'd only come back," she said.

"You're warming up to me," he says. "See? Just like I said."

"I'm trying to hear you out, you know, so you won't have to come back. We can finish all our business, right here."

"I think we've got to be friends, first," he says, "before our relationship can go any further."

"Listen—"

"Got something to show you," he says, interrupting her. Swinging his pack around, he unzips it and pulls out a piece of paper in a clear plastic sleeve. "Recognize me?"

Inside a square, black background, she sees the curve of the skull, then a white stripe, and then the twisted mass of brain, resting on its stem, which stretches white down the neck, all the way to the edge of the paper. The head is in profile, and it's obviously Scott—the small nose, the lips twisted in a smile, even then. It's as if his skull was cut in half.

"They gave it to me," he says, "after I got paid. I was thinking, you see, when all this was going on, when they took this—those are my thoughts working in there. You just have to imagine it all in color."

"How?" she says.

"Magnets," he says. "They just passed the forces through my head. Messed up the fillings in my teeth, I'll tell you that—when I lie down at night and there's more blood in my head I can feel my heart beating right here in my jaw."

"Didn't think fillings were magnetic," she says.

"Either way," he says, shrugging, "the doctors were real impressed."

"Well, pretty cool," she says, taking one last look at the picture, handing it back.

"Thing is," he says, "the thing of it is I got a favor to ask you. I been doing all those tests at the hospital, and now I've started to wonder if maybe they didn't put something in me. Implant, you know. Something I can't see."

"Why?"

"So I was wondering," he says, "if you'd let me go through your machine here, look for yourself, then tell me."

"No chance," she says.

"Worried about the danger?" he says. "I've done the MRI, the CAT scan, all kinds of X rays."

"So why not have your friends at the hospital check it out?" Ruth says.

Scott sets his pack on the floor, shifts his weight, tries to reach over his shoulder to scratch his back. He looks up, then down the empty terminal.

"Why not?" he says. "That's flat obvious. These are the people who put it in me, if there's anything in there. Why would they tell me?"

"Why would I tell you?" Ruth says.

"Why wouldn't you?"

"A million reasons," she says, and in that moment she believes she sees right through him. She decides to call his bluff. "You're daring me?" she says. "You think I won't do it, that's the only reason you're saying this."

"Let's do it, then," Scott says.

"Think I'm impressed?"

"I don't care if you're impressed." He sits on the conveyor belt, then swings his legs up and lies back, staring at the ceiling. "What about those video cameras up there?" he says.

"I'll let you in on a secret," she says. "They're fake, these one's here. Cheaper that way, and they still make people behave."

"Sure about that?"

"Would I risk my job if I wasn't?"

She steps on the switch and the conveyor belt comes alive. Scott's boots kick the rubber strips, then go through, his legs disappearing into the scanner. The screen is off; she turns it on, and it flickers, settles. Scott stares upward, his face calm, the backpack above his head, his body half in the machine, sliding farther. On the screen, his white femurs show, the wings of his pelvis, the bones disconnected, every muscle and sinew invisible.

The black rubber strips slip up his body, over his face; he winces, and then he's all the way inside, gone. She could call security now, make up some story they'd believe, and then they'd escort him away. She does not. Voices echo down the corridor, and she lifts her foot, stops the conveyor belt. Scott's ribs show on the screen, thin and white, bowed.

As she waits for the voices to fade, she's thinking of the dog, shaved and covered in words, and of the handcuffs, how they hold a space and then close it all the way down to spin right through themselves, open again, forgiving and ready to hold, patient. She's not sure if everything seems more unbalanced lately, or if she's just paying a different kind of attention, or if it's just so late and her mind is loosened, half asleep. She hopes Terrell is home now, asleep and safe; these nights there's no way to keep him there, no way of knowing. However things are spinning loose, she knows she's part of it—here she is, with this man inside the scanner. Even if she only wanted to call him out, face him down, it's too great a risk to have taken. She steps on the switch and the bones scroll by in the screen, the skull with its round eyes and terrible smile, the teeth thick and long, stretching all the way into the gums. There is no decent explanation, she knows, for what she is doing.

*   *   *

The Ambidextrist

Inside the scanner, the dark air rests heavily on Scott's body. He expected lights of some kind, a white strobe, but there's nothing like that; he breathes in, smells metal and plastic and leather. The belt beneath him slows and stops. He's surprised, delighted that Ruth went along with him. He'd made up the story, hoped to impress her with the idea, that was all, but then he'd seen how this was the start of something. She had to see it, too—now they had this connection between them, this thing they've done, this rule broken. She is so solid and talks so tough; she could set him straight, and he knows he can help her, too. He feels full of hope; he can sense her watching him. She must realize how honest he is, how ready he is for her to see straight through and inside him, how he has nothing to hide from her.

Twelve

Turncoat

Days pass. The lines of Terrell's tattoo are not solid, the edges a little unclear. It's all healed now, the scabs scratched off and the new skin grown over. The cross of the T isn't quite straight, as if it might fall off, but it's not going anywhere—it's definitely permanent. It rises up, wavering and sad, like it's sunken under water.

Terrell lets loose the waistband of his shorts, lets his shirt fall down again as the light changes and he crosses the street. He walks north, up Broad; glass bottles stand on the sidewalk, each holding forty ounces of air, just waiting to be broken and mixed with the glass that is everywhere, catching the sun. He's promised Ruth he'd stay out of this neighborhood. Across the street, two policemen wearing latex gloves handcuff a woman as she argues with them. Trash leans against cars— old box springs, shopping carts, stacks of newspapers. Some of the cars, missing doors, missing hoods and trunks, rest straight on their axles.

The windows of one has clear plastic duct-taped across them; the plastic bulges out, then in, as if someone is breathing inside.

Up ahead, three girls try to stay in the space cut by a jump rope; they spin and hop, clapping their hands, as two of their friends work the rope, all five of them chanting about Cinderella kissing a snake.

"Zina!" Terrell says. She's Swan's sister, her head shaved almost bald so she looks like a boy, a younger version of her brother. She leaps sideways, beyond the rope's reach, and steps closer.

"You seen Swan?" he says.

"Eric?" Zina wears a yellow dress with elastic all around the body, running shoes that used to be Swan's. A sticker on her dress says I HUGGED A CLOWN TODAY.

"He around?" Terrell says.

"No," she says. "Saw him at breakfast." Her feet twitch along the pavement, her mouth whispers numbers; behind her, the rope slaps down, whistles around, exerting its pull.

"All right," he says, and she's gone.

He walks out of the playground, past Temple, and takes a right on Diamond. It's hot; he stays close to the buildings, inside the stripe of shadow. Boys his own age are selling on corners, whistling signals back and forth. He's glad he doesn't live up here, like Swan and Darnay, though he might feel tougher if he did. People scream inside a house — voices barking, railing out windows, then muffled by walls, settling behind him. He tries to walk like he knows where he's going, what he's doing; he tries to make his face look bored. He wonders where Swan is now, and Darnay and John. Maybe they're down by the river, planning his test, or maybe Darnay has changed the order again. Terrell is tired of waiting; he hopes it comes soon.

Thirty feet away, he sees her. He's lucky to find her on the stoop, since he didn't want to knock on her door, make his searching obvious. Closer, he sees her hair is all caught up in red rubber bands, her head covered in clear plastic balls.

"Hey, Lakeesha."

She looks up, trying to place him, her eyelids low. She wears shorts, a track club T-shirt. She's barefoot, her toenails painted pink.

"What's up?" she says, acting unsurprised.

Sweat breaks out along his scalp, though he's still standing in the shade. He almost tells her his name, but for a moment it seems she recognizes him—as if, that day in the woods, she'd looked up, her eyes staring into the sky, and seen him sitting in the tree; as if she'd picked out his face, among the leaves.

"Can I sit down?" he says.

"If that's what you're fixing to do," she says.

"This your house, then?"

"No," she says. "Just kidding. I saw you all the way up the street, counting down the numbers."

"Wasn't," he says.

"What's your name?" she says. "Since you know mine."

"Terrell."

"Darrell?"

"Terrell."

"And I know you how?"

"I'm a friend of Eric Swan's," he says. "You remember him?"

"Oh, yes," she says, laughing. "So you know all about that."

"A little." Terrell wonders if anyone's in the house, listening, if the screen door might open and catch him right in the back.

"And you thought maybe you could come out here," she says, "and get some for yourself?"

The gold studs in her ears are so tiny he can hardly see them. Her thigh is close to his; he can feel the inch between them. She has a lighter patch of skin on her cheek, another on her forehead.

"You're looking at my necklace," she says.

"That's not why I came here," he says. "That's not what I thought." He hadn't been looking at her necklace, but now he leans closer. It's made of square, white beads, clustered together, holes drilled through them.

"They're my teeth," she says.

"What?" He looks at her mouth.

"My baby teeth. All the ones that fell out."

Terrell can't tell if the necklace is fake; he believes it is, but he's afraid to lean any closer or say what he thinks. He wants to reach out and take it in his fingers, roll the rough edges to test them. The teeth look too small, but he can't be sure. Looking at them, he remembers when his own teeth were loose, the exact feeling of fitting the tip of his tongue in the sharp hollow underneath, of pushing, of reaching with his fingers and twisting against the last skin that held.

"Look there," Lakeesha says, pointing. "That clothesline there — when I was a baby they clipped me to it and wheeled me out over the alley." She sticks out her pink tongue to emphasize her words. She waves her arms, bounces her legs. Her thigh touches his with a quick, silent slap and is gone again.

"Liar," he says.

"I'm just talking."

Terrell points to the electric and phone lines across the street; pairs of shoes hang all over it, dangling by their laces, thrown there by bullies and friends.

"Some good kicks up there," he says.

"Go after them and you'll get electrocuted," she says. "Sure thing. Saw a squirrel, once, where it chewed through to the line — it got fried, and its teeth were caught there, even after it was dead, so it was hanging down."

"I'd just get the shoes," he says. "Wouldn't chew on anything."

Her arms and legs seem longer, thinner than his; he wonders if she's taller. He almost wants to stand up with their backs and butts touching, facing away from each other, to measure. As he listens to her, he's thinking, he doesn't know why, of hanging from the monkey bars, that moment when his knuckles give out and his fingers still hold on, that sweet pain, the soles of his feet already pulsing, ready to slap down on the pavement below. A car alarm is going off, up the street. For a moment, Terrell worries Swan might walk by, see him here, but then he remembers it's Swan who asked him to come. Terrell sits next to Lakeesha, listening. He sees an old woman across the street, looking out from behind a window, standing perfectly still. Watching them. Dogs are barking somewhere close, sounding like they're being strangled. That's what Lakeesha's been talking about.

"Rottweilers back there killed a boy, one time," she says. "Come through the fence and chased him down, caught him by the school. Tore him up. Ate him. No one said a thing, police didn't come. Nothing."

"Right," Terrell says.

"Well, these ones here now are only replacements," she says, "but I think they're related to the ones who did it."

"Why'd you do it?" he says.

"What?"

"What you did with Swan." He feels the muscles tighten in the back of his neck, his shoulders. The reason he's here is to say Swan wants to see her again, but the sound of his friend's name annoys him when he says it.

Lakeesha just smiles. Her head turns, checking one corner, then the other. She flexes her toes over the concrete step; the pink of her nails disappears. When she speaks, her voice is soft, and she's still not looking at him.

"It's not the kind of thing I usually do," she says. "Just like that, for no reason."

"Why'd you do it, then?"

"To try it. Didn't you ever want to do something for no reason?"

111

"I don't know."

"I mean, that's a weird thing for me to do—I never did a thing like that before, probably wouldn't again. Not that he was a bad-looking boy. What'd he say about it?"

"Nothing," Terrell says.

"Enough to bring you here, I guess."

"He just told me you did it. That's all."

"Didn't say anything about me?"

"Not really."

"He was so nice and quiet," she says. "He asked me if I was all right, told me I didn't have to do it—but that's why I went there, you know?"

Terrell is thinking about her with Swan, out in the woods, and he's thinking about himself. Even if Lakeesha would go somewhere with him, right now, he wouldn't know where that would be, or what they would do, after. He wishes he was grown up, that he could sleep in the same bed with someone else, take their clothes right off, wake up and they would still be there, next to him.

"You know," he says. "I got to tell you something. That day in the woods—me and my friends were watching, the whole time. All that was Swan's plan. He set it up that way."

Lakeesha laughs out loud. She claps her hands together. "You came to tell me that?"

"Kind of," he says, surprised.

"You think I didn't know that? Think I trust that Darnay?"

"You didn't know," Terrell says. "You wouldn't have done it if you knew."

"That was part of the whole thing," she says. "And don't act like you didn't want to watch."

"Swan doesn't have anything good to say about you," he says. "If you care about that." He looks at her face, but he can't tell. "I have to get going," he says, standing.

"So why'd you come and find me?"

112

"I was walking by."

"You were counting down the numbers," Lakeesha says. "I saw you."

"I don't know why," Terrell says. "All right? I'll see you later."

"Hope so," she says.

☰ Thirteen

☰ Late

Finally, a night off. All Ruth knows is it's after midnight. Her watch rests face-down on the bedside table. Terrell hasn't come in yet, but that's no surprise. Holding a novel in her hands, she stares at the words without reading them. She lies atop the sheet, wearing pajama bottoms, a long-sleeved T-shirt; the skin of her feet, hands, and face is all that's showing.

The room is warm, the air close. The fan on the floor turns its head back and forth, having no effect. Reaching over, she pulls the plug and the fan swivels one more time, as if it takes that long to understand that the electricity is gone. This was her parent's bedroom. After they passed, she bought a new bed, tore down the curtains and bought new ones. She left the paint as it was, the eggshell cracks in the ceiling's plaster.

The table lamp casts her profile dark against the opposite wall.

114

With one hand, she makes the shadow of a dog, then takes hold of the book again, only to close and set it down. She switches off the light and lies back, thinking over her day, which had certainly not been typical.

Dwayne had come over. True, they'd talked about him visiting, sometime, but she knows how much connection talking has to things ever happening. He called early in the morning and showed up a few hours later.

He pulled up in an old Plymouth that was actually in pretty good shape—no dents or rust that she could see, though the paint was brown and that could hide it. All the widows on the street leaned out to get a look at him.

Ruth could see the shine of Dwayne's shoes from where she stood in the yard. He stepped out of the car, wearing a gray sweater tucked in and belted, as if trying to show off his paunch. She'd never seen him away from the airport, wearing anything but his uniform; she realized the same was true for him, and she was suddenly self-conscious about her skirt, about her calves and upper arms showing.

He was quick for his size, jogging down the sidewalk, not even breathing hard when he reached her. She hadn't been nervous until he was there—she was surprised at herself, and that only made her more flustered.

Calm and confident, Dwayne walked right in. The front room shrank around him. Up close, his sweater looked like it could be cashmere; the lines of his beard were sharp, but even the cashmere didn't hide the looseness under his chin. He circled the front room, asking questions.

"This your dad? This picture here must be your mama. Beautiful. And where's that brother you're always complaining about?"

She wonders what Terrell would make of Dwayne. Probably not much, though the boy is impossible to predict. She listens to the sirens,

115

the cats fighting outside. A man shouts something, far in the distance. Ruth rolls over, pulls up the sheet. Terrell is out there with all that, doing something; when she confronts him, he only stays out later. Usually she can just fall asleep, believing he'll be there in the morning, that he'll get home safely. Tonight she's having more trouble slowing her mind.

She almost turns on the radio to listen to the familiar, calming voices on KYW, but she does not. She thinks of Terrell, how he's getting to be a little man now, still embarrassed when she teases him about the hair in his armpits, the sparse whiskers on his chin. Summer's only a slight break from school, where things are never easy for him; they never contact her unless things are severely wrong, and Terrell's good at walking that line. She has her hopes, but her words always backfire—they only suggest things he's never considered doing, or new lies to tell her. Still, she has hopes for him, her brother. She knows there's nothing worse than seeing the limitations of those she loves—her parents, her family—and to see that they're not as smart or perceptive as she'd hoped, that their future is unclear, that people don't admire them. In a way, this is worse than realizing these things about herself, and in a way it is the same thing.

She can hear cars rushing along the expressway, in the still moments the sound carried across the river. The mirror above the dresser, tilted down, strokes dark shadows along the hardwood floor, catching the moonlight from outside. Her uniform hangs on the inside of the closet door, all its edges straight.

Tomorrow she'll see Dwayne at work; she wonders if he'll look different to her. Today he'd sat down and a kitchen chair creaked and swayed beneath his weight. He tried another, and it wasn't much better. He just laughed, hardly stopped talking. It turned out he knew more about Philadelphia than she expected, with his family stretching all the way back, in all directions. According to him, they fill a whole church congregation in West Philly.

He nervously slid the salt and pepper shakers along the tabletop; he lifted the curtains aside and squinted through the bars at the tangle of the yard. He complimented her curried chicken over couscous, got her to name the spices.

"Reminds me of the house I grew up in," he said. "Same house I live in now, actually. It's just me and my mother. She's still got a few years left—they sure won't be quiet ones."

The water glass looked small in his hand. The bulk of him was reassuring, as if he couldn't go anywhere too quickly. He asked her questions about herself, too, he didn't just talk—and the airport was never mentioned. He's thirty-two, younger than she is; that surprised her a little, not that it matters. As the afternoon went on, even the stud in his nose began to seem like less of an affectation. He did an imitation of his niece dribbling a basketball that shook the whole house, almost took the pans from their hooks on the walls. It had been a long time since the kitchen held so much laughter.

Now Ruth hears the back door open, then footsteps, jars clinking against each other in the door of the refrigerator, the faucet running. After a pause, Terrell climbs the stairs, stepping on every other one. Then the door swings open, the hinges faintly whining. She feels a change in the shape of the air, his body in the room.

Fairly often, he still climbs into her bed, in the middle of the night. This started when he was a little boy, and it hasn't stopped. She never teases him about it, since she knows he wouldn't do it if he could prevent himself, if he wasn't frightened. She feels the wedge of air as he lifts the sheet.

Outside, all the sirens have gone silent. Ruth does not let him know she's awake. The curtains sway a little, in the breeze through the screens, making it feel like the bed is moving slightly, afloat. She sniffs,

117

The Ambidextrist

but she smells no alcohol, no smoke of any kind; just the sweetness of his sweat, his breath. She rolls over, as smoothly and quietly as she can, and looks into his face. His eyes are closed, jerking behind his smooth lids. His mouth is slightly open, his hands folded under his cheek. He is already asleep.

Fourteen

Equestrians

Ray is not in the hidden garden, and that is all right, since it is not a bad place to be alone. It calms Scott, sitting here, surrounded by all the carved wooden figures, the pond reflecting the sky and the leaves above. Being here makes him feel hopeful, despite everything; it helps him believe that people find beauty in unexpected places, that if he holds it inside someone will eventually find it. He spent this morning at the hospital, doing smell and taste tests. Lisa Roberts told him the scratch-and-sniff booklets—gasoline, root beer, grass, everything—cost a hundred dollars apiece. After that, he'd swilled mouthfuls of liquid from paper cups, spitting them out and saying whether they tasted sweet, bitter, or sour. Now his mouth is dry; he purses his lips, licks them.

Standing, he heads out of the garden, under the trees, still keeping an eye out for Ray. It's been a week since Scott last stayed over at the

119

waterworks, and he needs a good night's sleep; he never sleeps better than with his friend beside him.

It's late afternoon. Roller skaters and people on bicycles swerve past as he heads along Kelly Drive, toward the museum.

When he reaches the azalea garden, he looks up at the statues along the slanted hill, the huge building striped with shadows. Worn flowers drop their petals on the ground; Sitting down, he pulls off his boots, then his socks. He stands close to the bushes, in their shadows, the grass soft and cool between his toes. It's then that he catches a glimpse of the horse—in his peripheral vision, beyond where a bride and groom are having their picture taken. He tries to keep it away by ignoring it, he hurries to pull his boots back on, but the horse keeps coming.

Its long, flat head is like some kind of hammer, lips unfolding, bent outward to show its teeth. The eyes are wide, white circles around the edges. Dark lines of flies are shaken free and form again along the trembling muscles, where the veins fork across the horse's chest. The thick smell of the thing is stirred by its tail, straight into his nostrils, mixed with the sweat, the leather of the saddle. The top of Scott's head only reaches the horse's shoulders. His heart speeds blood all through his body, out along his fingertips. The horse works its teeth sideways, grinding them, trying to spit out the metal bit under its tongue. The hair on the its leg overlaps the hoof, each hair thick and sharp; the metal shoes are nailed straight in, he knows—that's part of what makes horses so mean.

It stomps its foot and Scott jumps back, flinching, trying to keep his eyes open. He pulls on his boots, his socks in his hands, and begins walking away up the slope, swinging his arms, not looking back.

"Hey," the policeman calls. "Everything all right?"

The horse's metal shoes ring on the pavement as Scott begins to pick up his pace. He moves around the front of the museum, across Vine Street.

Equestrians

He drifts to the left, putting a tree trunk between them; he fights off the urge to run. The horse's eyes are like hot marbles rolling around his body, just inside his skin. Looking back, he sees the thing standing motionless, the policeman still watching.

Scott trips over a pile of cans, where someone has torn open a plastic trash bag and strewn everything around, then pulls his jacket more tightly around himself, as if that might make him smaller, harder to see. When he kicks at the squirrels they double back, shoot up trees, then chitter at him from the branches above. Closer to the river, he heads into the bushes; dark shapes move close by; he smells the thin, harsh crack smoke as it slips through the air, past him.

Once he sees the river, the water sliding along, he feels a little better. He sits on the ground, his back against a tree, and begins thinking of other times, like last winter, before he ever thought of coming to Philadelphia. It had been out in North Dakota, where Chrissie told their ride to pull over and let them out, miles from any town, all because she said they'd passed a sign that said HORSEBACK RIDES. They walked back the way they'd come, in the cold, hunks of steam huffing from their mouths, and he'd known they'd be stuck there for hours, watching cars accelerate at the sight of them—hitchhiking was always easier in a town, where they could corner someone in a parking lot, hold a door open for an old man, or start a conversation, stir up pity.

What it was, set right out there on the interstate, was a half-assed animal park; a small herd of shivering deer lined one fence, watching with the sad look of hope. The whole prairie dog town appeared to be in hibernation.

An old woman came to the door of the house, after Chrissie knocked long enough, and then she led them out to the barn, the ridges of mud solid beneath her feet, holding a cigarette in her gloved hand. The roof of the barn was covered in weather vanes: cows and roosters and wrought-iron arrows, some others so broken it was impossible to tell what they were supposed to be. There he'd stood in his

121

cowboy boots, while Chrissie wore nylon moonboots, stripes on the side, laces crisscrossing, arched soles made to walk on barren planets. He had to go first.

It started out well enough, the horse solid beneath him, his feet in the stirrups, but as soon as he let go of the fence the thing stepped backward, hunched its spine, bucked sideways. He kicked one boot free and went off the other way, landed on all fours, crawled out under the fence.

"Overreaction," Chrissie said.

"That horse's always been so gentle," the woman said.

And it was, once Chrissie was in the saddle. She leaned close, along the horse's neck, smiling and whispering in its ear, her hair—red, verging on pink, she swore she never dyed it—showing around the edges of the hat he'd made from the cutoff arm of a sweatshirt. She rode circles inside the corral, the saddlehorn poking right into her stomach, the toes of the moonboots not quite fitting in the stirrups. She rode on, and her laughter, which usually made him so happy, began to give him a headache.

Out there, he could see the sun and the moon in the gray sky, and he could not tell which was which. The old woman opened the gate and Chrissie rode off across the snow-swept ground, toward a stand of bare trees a hundred yards away. The woman began to tell him about the summer, and he didn't ask questions, for he wanted to believe everything she said about the time when everything was visible, warm and available, when all the children came running to feed the deer. Finally, Chrissie returned. At a distance, it was impossible to separate her silhouette from the horse's, as if the two of them were one creature; it was a relief when he could see the edges between them, the thick air chuffing from their mouths.

"Try it again, Scott," she said. "I wore him out a little now. I told him you were really all right."

He could never stay mad at her, though he wanted to waste no time getting away from where she could see him and the horse together. Later, she talked about how her unborn child had felt the horse, that the child would ride before it would ever walk. She even bought a book all about horses, and carried it around with her, just like a little girl. *Natural Horse-Man-Ship*, it was called, written by a handsome man named Pat Parelli. Scott sometimes wondered if she ever read it, or if she only looked at the pictures.

He read it, all he could. He pretended to disdain it, but sometimes—when she fell asleep and her fingers loosened, or if she left it behind at the table while she went to the ladies' room in some diner—he'd sneak a few lines, pick up some ideas. That's where he learned about smiling. He learned that the two-legged way people walk scares horses, reminds them of some distant predator—you wanted to maintain that fear while at the same time forging a certain trust. The whites of a horse's eyes, when they showed around the edges, meant they were anxious. Back then, he wondered what that meant about people, if anything; he began to think some of the same strategies might hold. The smile, the walk. Instead of predator and prey, everyone could be partners.

Scott stands, leaning against the tree to stretch his legs, then walks upriver, under the overpass, and toward the waterworks. The construction workers are gone for the day, leaving behind the scaffolding and a few big pieces of machinery. Bulldozers, dump trucks. The fence has been mended, but there's still a place where it can be unclipped; he slides underneath, clips it back behind him. During the day there's a security guard—now it's after five, unguarded. Scott needs quality sleep, and tonight he'll rest here with Ray, even if he has to drift off alone and be awakened by the touch of the old man's back, pressed against his in the darkness.

He goes under the metal skeleton of scaffolding, climbs through the open window. Inside, his footsteps echo, his own breath surrounds his ears. Shadows gather into darkness, up above; around him, there's only enough light to find where Ray's rolled-up piece of foam rubber is hidden. The workmen are already spending time inside, so he'll have to be more careful, be certain to get up before their arrival at dawn.

Scott sits down, pulls off his boots, then rests his head on his pack, his jacket flat on top of him. He stares straight to the ceiling high above, then closes his eyes. As he rests in the darkness, waiting, he repeats the words of Pat Parelli, softly, to himself:"Good, better, best, never let it rest. Get your good better and your better best."

That horse in North Dakota had seen the fear in him, had read his tentative touch. This is what it is, he knows it now—that horses are all his fears, all the things he doesn't know. That might be horse sense—being prepared for any possibility, confident—and it is similar to being ambidextrous, or even beyond that. He is learning.

Fifteen

Cowards and Weaklings

Terrell and Swan are playing on the basketball court in the park along the river. There are no nets on the hoops, and the rims are bent down a little, so they look like eyes, staring and squinting, daring the shooter. The boys shoot with a tennis ball they've found; when Terrell throws it over the backboard, they search the tall grass until they have to give up.

It's dusk. Those lights that aren't broken flicker on, high above, but it's not dark enough for them to do any good. People and dogs walk the paths. Terrell looks up; it's impossible to read anyone's expression, their faces full of shadows.

"Let's go," Swan says. "It's getting late."

Terrell follows him around the chain-link fence, through the hedge. Their bare arms touch and they both lean away, walking. The air is moist and warm; it smells like, somewhere, plastic is burning.

"You seen Lakeesha?" Swan says.

125

"Have you?"

"No, after what you told me."

"Can't blame you," Terrell says.

"I can't believe it, though."

"Believe it."

"She didn't seem that way."

"She is that way," Terrell says, "and I haven't seen her."

The weeds give way to the sharp stones that hold the tracks in place; the train is parked there, long and dark, all straight edges. Climbing up first, Terrell balances on the coupling where the cars hitch together. The train creaks, but doesn't start to roll. He jumps down, on the river side, Swan behind him.

"Seems like you don't want to talk about her."

"Who?" Terrell says.

"Lakeesha."

"Why would I? I'm not the one that did her—I'm not anything like that."

"Whatever."

"I can't change what she said." Terrell looks over at Swan's eyes, wide open, believing. Past him, upriver, the huge lighted letters revolve around the square top of the Peco Building: 9:02 ENERGY FOR TOMORROW 9:03. They keep circling, right above Swan's head.

There's no wind and the water is perfectly still and flat; plastic bottles and paper cups rest everywhere on the surface with sludge circled around them, holding them in place. The water looks solid, like a vacant lot, as if they could slide down the concrete bulkhead and walk across to the other side. They sit silently, feet dangling, the water five feet below. Terrell wishes they could just stay like this and not be waiting for something to happen, for someone else to come.

"Worried about school?"

"That's more than a month away."

Faint headlights slide down the expressway, across the river; a few cars peel off and snake along the South Street Bridge, point at the boys for a minute, then swing past.

They hear John's footsteps before they see him. The gray sky silhouettes his round head, hair flattened along his skull by a hat he's no longer wearing.

"How's your dog, brother?"

That's how they always greet him, now. John doesn't answer. His face has a slippery shine. The air is thick and still, more humid every minute. He looks back the way he's come, as if someone might be following, then sits down.

"What's up with Darnay?"

"Not yet."

"Man, my parents," John says.

"What about them?"

"Nothing."

They sit silently for a minute, the river not moving at all.

"I almost forgot," Swan says, reaching into his pocket. He holds up a blunt, the thin cigar hollowed out and the buds forced inside. "Guy gave it to me for a favor I did. Could smoke it right now."

"Let's wait for Darnay," John says.

"He might not show."

"He's not afraid."

"Didn't say he was." Swan turns to Terrell. "Smoke?" He has a book of matches flapping open in his other hand.

"Go ahead."

The flame lights up Swan's smooth face, then dims. Terrell stands. He smells the tobacco, mixed with the sweetness of the pot. He wonders why Swan didn't mention the blunt before, there in his pocket the whole afternoon.

"You're going to cough," Terrell tells John. John doesn't cough. He passes it back to Swan.

Terrell steps farther away, behind them, thinking. He had seen

127

her, no matter what he told Swan. Lakeesha. Twice. He'd gone looking for her, pretended it was a mistake, but she knew better. She made
him buy her a water ice, circled all kinds of words around him, tall
tales and laughter. When he ate too fast and the ice burned his throat,
she put her warm, sticky hands there, a gentle strangle until he felt
better.

"I know how to smoke a blunt, homeboy," John says. His voice
sounds almost black; not quite. It wavers, false. Out on the expressway,
the cars thin, headlights spread out.

The second time Terrell had seen Lakeesha, she'd even asked
after Swan. Terrell just said Swan didn't want to have anything to do
with her. "You're a little jealous when you say his name—you got no
right to that," she said. "So what if he said what you say, called me
what you say he did." Terrell just smiled, looked at all the twists in her
hair, took in the thick scent of her, close. Just then, she was worth
lying for.

John throws a stone in the water, then laughs at the splash. Swan
does the same, then pretends to throw another one and John bursts
out laughing when he can't wait for the splash any longer. The river
is black; the dark water betrays no ripples, no currents. Terrell
walks farther along the bulkhead, listening. He picks out words—
"stupid," "exactly," "him?"—and feels them pointing in his direction. Terrell's thinking how John has always been at the bottom
of their group—he's white, and slow, and tries too hard. John's done
his test, though, like Swan. It's unclear if there will ever be enough
tests; there's Darnay's, then Terrell's, then one they'll all do. That
might be the last one. Maybe not. The four of them have hung
together so long because it's easier, safer. Between them, though,
they pair up in different ways, at different times, to protect themselves.

"Isn't that right, Terrell?" Swan shouts.

"Right," he says. This sets them to laughing again, he doesn't know why.

His hands are dirty, from climbing between the cars of the train. The gravel looks cool and white beneath the moon; when he drags his palms along the stones they feel greasy, not cool at all.

At first, the honking sounds like a car alarm, but it follows no rhythm. It pauses, and Terrell hears a voice shouting, perhaps even his name.

"Hear that?" he says.

"What?" say Swan and John.

Now the headlights are visible, thirty feet away. The three boys walk toward them. It's a relief to Terrell, getting the two of them in motion. They're still giggling, pushing each other. Terrell walks ahead. The lights shine straight in his eyes, then switch off. Blue spots float, lagging just as he brings the car into focus, fading so he can see again.

"Late," Darnay says. "I'm late." The driver's door is open, and the yellow light shines out, along the pale spots on his arms, where he's ripped off scabs. There's a comb in his hair, sticking out like a plastic wing. Blue. He slams the car door and the yellow light goes out.

They shake all around; John and Swan both shake Terrell's hand again, as if they haven't been together for the last half hour.

"These two are stoned," he says to Darnay.

"Man," John says.

"How?" says Swan.

"Dude left it idling, outside the liquor store, so I just took it," Darnay says, proud. "Someone's looking for it right now, I'll tell you that."

It's a Toyota or Mazda, four doors, idling rough, rusted through behind the tires. Darnay slaps the hood and the clap is deep, surprising. High above, on the lighted billboard, the Marlboro horses run lathered and wild.

"It's not like I brought it down here just to show your sorry asses. You getting in or what?"

"Shotgun," John says, going around the other side of the car, opening the door. Terrell and Swan climb in the back. Darnay shifts into reverse, eases out. He turns the wheel the wrong way and they just miss a metal post.

Every parked car is a waiting collision. Those that are moving all have bad intentions. Darnay takes a corner too sharply and the back tire jumps a curb. Still, it is a different feeling, riding, moving without trying. The whole thing is so small, low to the ground. John is the only one of them whose family owns a car. His parents have two.

"What now?"

"We're just going to drive around?"

"That's not much of a test."

"We'll see what it is."

A police car passes, two blocks away, and they all stop talking. The inside of the car smells like dust and Lysol. Rusty chains are tangled thick on the floor of the backseat, beneath Terrell's and Swan's feet. A roll of duct tape, squashed flat, rests with two orange plastic mugs from Wawa.

"Radio's already been stolen," John says.

"What's that?" Swan says, leaning forward, pointing through the windshield.

A bicycle crosses the headlights, its edges uneven, all kinds of things hanging off it. The rider looks about to tip over or fall off.

"Follow him," Terrell says. He wants something to happen, something more.

Darnay wheels left, accelerates. The old man's skinny ass switches back and forth; the bicycle's rearview mirrors catch the headlights and return them, sharp. The boys are all talking now, together, trying to get the windows down to shout.

"Can't stand him."

"We're on your ass!"

The old man's not looking back, not at all. He's standing to pump harder, his feet going around and around, his shirttail flapping out like a cape. He swoops down an alley, left, and Darnay can't stop in time.

"Go back!"

"It's one-way."

They go around the block, but they can't see where the man has gone. They roll slowly down the alley, hanging out the windows.

"We'll get you, don't worry!"

"Maybe he's hiding behind the Dumpster."

"Forget it," Darnay says. "We got to do something better than follow some sick old dude. We can catch him another time."

They turn onto Market Street, past the neon signs of the porn theater—LIVE SEXY FUN—and then coast through a yellow light, only to be caught by the next one. Tall buildings stretch up on either side; their tops bend in, swaying overhead, so it seems the car is driving down the bottom of a trench. Another light turns red.

"Don't run it," John says.

Ten feet away, a white girl stands in a short skirt and sandals, waiting for the bus. Her legs are thick, with black stockings pulled up to her dimpled knees. Her light hair is pulled back, up off her neck. She's probably ten years older than they are.

"Hey, baby," John says, and before they can even laugh at him she's stepping closer to the car, looking inside.

"Baby?" she says. "You're just little boys."

She turns her back to them, steps toward the Plexiglas bus shelter. Just as Terrell's thinking of something to say, the car behind them starts honking and they have to pull through the green light.

131

"Damn," Swan says.

"Bitch," John says, his voice tough again.

"Circle back," Terrell says.

"Don't try to get in on my test," Darnay says, but he goes back around the block.

"Pull up close," Terrell says. "Stop here."

He feels his weight on the ground again, his feet slow. She isn't facing him, then turns and looks past him, searching for the bus.

"Listen," he says.

There's no one around, not within a block, hardly any cars passing. She ignores him.

"Listen," he says again, closer. He reaches out to touch her. As she turns away, he already has hold of her wrists. One, then the other. Her arms are thicker than his, but he's stronger. She screams something and he's dragging her back to the car, not knowing what he wants and still forcing her inside, into Swan. He kicks himself in after.

Darnay hits the gas and the door slams shut on its own. Lights spin down through the windows, sliding away, and Terrell's face is pressed into the warm vinyl of the seat, his nose bent. The three of them tangle across the backseat—him, Swan, the girl. She's screaming; he tries to quiet her and she bites his hand, catches a finger in her teeth. It's too loud; he wants to roll up the windows, but can't. He gets her under him, surfaces.

"Out past the museum," he says, gasping.

Swan's getting kicked by her. Darnay's looking straight through the windshield, and so is John, not helping at all. Terrell tries to think ahead. Her breathing, higher than his, is coming fast; at least she's stopped screaming. Swan has her wrists, and Terrell takes the duct tape and circles them, her hands pressed together, fingers clawing at each other. She's sitting between them, her shoes kicked loose. Terrell pulls off one stocking, loops it, gets it around her head, over her eyes. She tries to reach it with her hands.

132

"Don't," he says.

"What do you want?" she says. "Money?"

No one answers her. No one knows.

"Shut up," Terrell says. "No one use their real name."

"I'm going to start screaming again."

"No one would hear you."

"We haven't gone that far."

"I'll tape your mouth," he says.

It's hard to tell if people on the sidewalk are staring, if the cars around them are chasing or just moving along in their lanes. Darnay slows, taking a corner, and she goes for the door, scratching Terrell, catching him in the face with her elbow. Pain echoes in his cheekbone; he holds her still again. She kicks the back of Darnay's seat and they swerve. No one sees it, there are no other cars close by. They're past the museum now, and the road is darker.

"Do that again, and," Darnay says, but after a minute it seems he won't say what will happen if she does.

"I won't use my real name, either," she says.

"So what?"

"So nothing."

Terrell pulls on the loose end of the duct tape, and the raspy sound quiets her. In the headlights of oncoming cars, he watches her face—the tiny blond hairs on her upper lip, in front of her ears. Her teeth bite her lip, let go; her mouth is moving with hardly any sound.

"Did you say 'cowards and weaklings'?" he says.

"I'm being quiet," she says.

"She can see through that blindfold," John says, turning.

"Not very well," she says.

"Shut up," Terrell says. He looks down at her bare white feet, atop the tangled chain. The blindfold makes her seem more dangerous, as if not being able to see gives her more time to think.

"Janine Draper," Swan says, the wallet in his hand.

"How much she have?"

"Four bucks and a bunch of bus tokens."

"Bus?" Darnay says. "We're driving."

"Sure are," John says.

They drive into Fairmount Park, up a long hill, no one around. Terrell flexes his fingers; his hands are sore. In the daylight he'll have scabs marking the shape of her teeth. Janine. Her lips are going again, silent curses. He wonders where Darnay really got this car, if it's even stolen, why he got to choose his own test and why John and Swan aren't acting stoned anymore. Terrell can hardly recognize the way he's thinking, as if he's the one that's stoned. He likes it, this excitement, and he doesn't like it. He wonders what his friends are thinking, what they believe will happen next.

The moon shines through the windows as the car swoops around overgrown lawns, up and down hills, past baseball diamonds and all the old mansions, some with fences surrounding them, some with plywood in their windows.

"You still got the gun?" John says to Darnay.

" 'Course. Like I'd get rid of it."

Terrell wonders where it is—in the glove compartment? Under the seat? Would they get it out? Did it have bullets in it and would it fire straight? Crooked? Explode in their hands? They roll past picnic tables, past garbage cans tipped over and bent, then into the trees again. He thinks he sees a white face flash, looks back and there's only the heavy leaves, motionless in the sticky moonlight. The girl whispers to herself. John and Darnay and Swan are laughing, and he laughs along with them. He recognizes the same mansion once, then it comes around again.

"Where we going?" Swan says.

"We're getting there," Darnay says.

They circle, none of them sure what to do next, afraid to name possibilities for fear they'll dare each other to carry them out.

Cowards and Weaklings

"What are the chains for?" she says.

No one answers. Terrell can smell her perfume and her sweat. He presses himself against the door, so their bare thighs aren't touching. Maybe she thinks they're going to hang her up somewhere, from a tree limb or the rafters of an old barn—not to hurt her, but just to leave her there, screaming until her voice gives out. Or maybe she is thinking they'll lead her farther into the woods, leave the car behind, make her take off her clothes and throw each piece into the tree branches. Then they'll just stand on every side and look at her, pale in the moonlight. And maybe she'll run, barefoot, and they'll chase her without a word, silent, careful not to lose her.

It is too quiet for that now, the trees too still. The car circles under them. Terrell can see straight through the gray leaves in some places, to the black trunks, where they divide and twist into branches. Ahead, the road is almost white under the moon. He's the one who started this, and he'd liked it then. He rolls down his window and the ragged air fights its way inside, warm around them.

"Pull over," he says.

"Don't think this counts as your test," Darnay says. The car rolls to a stop.

"I don't," Terrell says. Opening his door, he drags her out behind him. She refuses to walk, collapses on the road. Swan's door opens, then Darnay's.

"Stay inside." Terrell lets go and steps away from her. He walks farther from the car, by himself; twenty feet away, he can no longer hear it idling. At once, a rush of crickets soften the air around him. He sees lights through the trees—cars below, on Kelly Drive, following the curves of the river.

Turning, he walks back toward the car, around where she sits, shivering, both feet now bare. He sits next to Swan, slams the door. He drops her shoes out the open window.

"Drive," he says.

135

As they roll away, they look back at her. Hands still taped together, she pulls the blindfold down, uncovering her eyes. She watches them go.

"What if she gets the license plate?"

"What if she does?"

Sixteen

Jealousy

Scott waits for the sunrise, sitting in an upstairs bedroom, in one of the abandoned mansions in the park—some rich people's summer home, a hundred years before. He'd come in through a window, crack vials underfoot, footsteps quiet as he could make them as he went around a dead bird, chose this room. It wasn't until later that he heard the voices, other people in the house, arguments and scuffling, car doors slamming outside, engines approaching and driving away. He has not been able to sleep, and it wasn't for fear that he would be found, but because the arguments made him anxious—he wanted the voices to slow and settle, for the people to understand each other.

Now the sun rises, and the people are finally gone. Scott climbs out of the house, crawls across the untended lawn. Walking, he passes long, dark cars as they idle. The black men inside ignore him; they hold binoculars to their eyes, scanning a distant line of trees where he can see no motion at all. He heads in the other direction, walking ten

137

minutes through the forest paths without seeing another person. He crosses a road, walks under a tattered LOST DOG sign that hangs from a telephone pole. The morning is warm, with just a trace of wind. He feels wired, restless.

Back in the trees, he picks up his pace, trying to move without making a sound. He enters a clearing where all different-sized birds gather. Robins bigger than sparrows, pigeons the largest of all. A flash of red blazes past him, right over his shoulder, and he spins but only glimpses the bird; it does not slow.

Scott hurries onward. As he recognizes the entrance, the tunnel of bushes, he begins to take off his boots, then does not. He doesn't want to surprise Ray, if he is here. He lets the tiny bells, hanging from fishing line, ring out as he approaches.

Ray sits with his legs crossed, one hand on his knife's handle, its blade stuck into the ground. Turning his head, he sees Scott; his white beard circles his smile.

"My man!" He uncrosses his legs, stretches them out straight. "Where you been sleeping? Trying to make me jealous?"

"Look like you're meditating," Scott says. "Cross-legged and everything."

Ray wears brown polyester slacks, a sharp crease down the front, and a yellow-and-orange striped shirt with the sleeves rolled up. Thick veins fork along the bones of his dark forearms. In front of him, in the polished dirt, is a mosaic; loose piles of broken glass and bottle caps rest close to his knees.

"Vegetating's another word," he says. "Just getting a little sorted out, here. You know, you're starting to look like you really live on the streets. You blend right in—that's a good talent to have. The other half of it's knowing when to use it, of course, knowing the times."

"What?"

"To disappear," Ray says. "Seriously, you look terrible—except for those new specs. Those I like."

Jealousy

"Didn't sleep much last night," Scott says, touching the glasses frames.

"Well, have a seat, have a seat."

There is just enough space between Ray's back and the bushes for Scott to squeeze through. He sits in the runnerless rocking chair, its stunted legs stuck into the ground, the shallow pond stretching out at his feet. The morning light reflects in the water, and from the broken glass and mirrors, the pieces of metal, the silverware. The chicken-bone skeletons are dull, polished; they absorb the light.

"I been here before," he says. "Plenty of times. I've known about it. I knew it was yours."

"I never said it was a secret," Ray says.

"But you never told me."

"You never asked about it."

Scott looks away, to where silver batteries stand in a line; he knows the old man believes the sun might revive them. Closer, a string of red ants files across the cracked dirt, finding their way.

"That's because," he says, "I wanted you to just tell me, to want to, you know? I told you my secrets. I told you everything."

"You're tired," Ray says. "You're here, now. There's really nothing to say." He waves his hand over his garden. "Here you are."

Scott sits back, closing his eyes. "Saw a cardinal this morning," he says. "Think I did, anyway. I didn't think colored animals could live here anymore, like they either went somewhere else or changed over to gray and brown. Ever ate a bird, round here?"

"Would if I could catch one," Ray says, not looking up. "Fish I can catch, squirrels sometimes. Rats."

"Pull on my other leg," Scott says, holding it out. "You don't eat rats."

"You wouldn't?"

"A squirrel, maybe."

"Now what's the difference between a rat and a squirrel?"

139

"Plenty."

"They're both rodents. About the same size. If you got hold of a squirrel, circled a finger real tight at the base of their tail, and pulled to the tip, taking off all the fuzz, what would you have left in your hand?"

"A whip-tailed squirrel," Scott says. He kicks off his cowboy boots, peels his socks loose, bends his toes. "Also, squirrels got a different kind of cheeks on them."

"I've been considering those Canadian geese," Ray says, pointing a cigarette toward the river, which is distant, invisible. He blows smoke through his nose. "Where they gather up near Strawberry Mansion Bridge. There's a bird I'd like to eat—I could plow right into them on my bike; I mean, I almost hit them anyway. A regular Thanksgiving dinner, one of those. Leftovers for a month." Ray's knuckles are thicker than his fingers, pale palms flashing as he talks. "Could even take them on a hook and line, if you got the bait right."

The pool surrounded by all the carved animals, reflects the sliding leaves, the smiling faces glued to spoons. Scott imagines a goose caught on the end of a line, flying back and forth like a wild kite.

"People do things for all kinds of reasons," he says.

"Expect me to argue with that?" Ray says. "Thing is, about those geese—they're powerful. You'd have to wring their necks fast. And if people were around, you know, that'd be another complication."

"This place," Scott says. "Even the first time, I knew. There's no reason, except it's beautiful. That's why you made it, went to all this trouble, beyond everything."

Ray just looks up at him and smiles.

"How you feeling?" he says. "You look tired, my man, and your talk is getting a little out there. You want to take a little nap, maybe? Could lay down right here and I'll watch you. Watch your stuff."

Scott shakes his head. He listens to the garden, the wind in the trees high above, the sound of leaves.

Jealousy

"Everyone's got to work at something other than eating and sleeping," Ray says, "the way I see it. To give them a reason to eat and sleep. I just wanted a place to relax—this one place, where no one can question me. I'm the best at making this place."

"Right," Scott says.

"And I never meant it to be a secret, just hid it in case someone would mess with it. I wanted to share it. Maybe find some young person to help me."

"Exactly," Scott says. "I think I could get a feel for that."

"I was thinking someone younger," Ray says.

"A kid?" Scott says. "That'd be a mistake."

"How's that?"

"About the only thing meaner than a horse is a kid," Scott says.

"Always thought they were gentle, mostly. Horses."

"You're wrong about that."

"And boys are gentle," Ray says. "Really, they are, once they get settled."

"False," Scott says. "Even the ones that grow up all right, they were mean kids. I'd have wrecked that garden in a split second, no doubt, when I was a boy. Done a lot worse. That's all I'm saying here."

He looks away, trying to bring his voice down. On the far side of the garden, two ravens are fighting over a candy wrapper, throwing it in the air and hopping after it, their black feathers catching the sun.

"I mean," Ray says. "A young boy's about the best friend you can have. They're curious, and they really appreciate things, you know. They're so smooth. They talk straight."

"Sometimes," Scott says, "something, when it draws you like that, you got to wonder if you're getting pulled in somewhere you shouldn't go. That's when you step back."

"You know something about that?" Ray says.

"I been surprised in my life."

141

"We're talking about boys here," Ray says. "Little boys."

"Exactly," Scott says. "It's been so long since you've been one, you can't remember."

"And you can?"

"Closer than you."

"Now you're the one who sounds jealous," Ray says.

"Compared to what?"

"That's what you said about me."

"When did I say you sounded jealous?"

"When I asked where you slept last night."

"I did not," Scott says.

"You acted like it."

"Like what?"

"Like you thought I was jealous."

"Listen," Scott says. "I just don't want anything to happen to you. All right?"

"And why not?"

"I don't know," Scott says; they've been speaking quickly, and it feels strange to pause. "It'd be good to know you're around, I guess."

"In the future," Ray says, his voice lower.

"Right," Scott says. "What you got planned for the future?"

"Laundromat, maybe."

"Dark or light?" Scott says. "We could split the coins."

The tightness has eased in the air around them. Ray is kneeling, clapping his hands together.

"Too nice a day," he says, "to go inside, just yet."

"You'll be here a while?" Scott stands, still barefoot. "It's all right then, if I drop off for half an hour or so?"

Ray just waves his hand over his garden, as if to say he has plenty to occupy him.

Grass grows behind the rocking chair. Laying his pack under his head, Scott settles down. When he awakens, he'll go to the bank or

Jealousy

somewhere else with a rest room, sponge himself down, be clean again. The shadows of leaves slide across his face, flashes of light through his eyelids. As he lets himself drift off, he listens to Ray whistling, high notes and low. He wishes the old man would come and lie down beside him, just for a little while.

Seventeen

= Tested

A few days later, Scott crosses the parkway, then over 676, cars slipping beneath his feet. He heads south, parallel to the river, through neighborhoods of row houses. Mirrored buildings rise on his left, reflecting each other, multiplying the heat.

The row houses are narrow, one room across, sharing walls, holding each other together. The whole street is in shadow, dark and hot, the sun bright overhead between the rooftops. From his pack, Scott takes half a loaf of bread. Two vitamins rattle in a bottle. He swallows them dry, then tears up a slice of bread, rolls the pieces into balls, and folds another slice around them, choking it down that way. It feels like someone is watching him, but when he looks around, he's all alone. And he's thirsty. Air conditioners drip on him, water evaporating as it hits the sidewalk.

He cuts through a parking lot and the attendant stands in his tiny windowed booth, about to say something before deciding to sit back down. Heat seeps from steam grates in the sidewalk, bending the air. Passing cars only stir it around. The river below the bridge is still, darkly reflecting, holding a piece of tree trunk half submerged. A train rests on the tracks, motionless and rusty, both head and tail curving beyond where he can see.

"Scott!"

Someone is calling his name. He looks over the railing, right at the edge of the river, sixty feet below. It's Terrell, waving for him to come, shouting his name again.

"Scott! Got something to tell you!"

The stairway jerks itself down, back and forth; Scott takes the steps two at a time, as if the boy might disappear before he gets there. But he still stands on the gravel path, waiting, a carton of lemonade in one hand.

"Glad to see you, Terrell," Scott says. "You remembered my name."

"You tell me every time I see you."

"Probably do. Spare a drink?"

"Finish it."

Scott gulps down the last sweet swallows, then crushes the carton in his hands. Terrell's watching him; the boy seems taller, as if he's grown in the few weeks Scott's known him.

"Those wristbands made out of socks?"

"You're one to talk," Scott says. "With all your clothes two sizes too big."

Terrell shrugs his thin shoulders inside his T-shirt, which hangs halfway to his knees. His knees are hidden by his shorts.

"What's Ruth getting up to?"

"Nothing."

Scott can't figure out the way Terrell's looking at him—all anticipation, just staring and then looking away.

"She's got a boyfriend now," Terrell says. "She's working."

"Great," Scott says, both wanting and not wanting to know more.

145

He looks closely at Terrell's face. "You got to go with the flow and flow with the go, know what I mean?"

"What?" Terrell says.

"You feel all right?"

"Yeah."

"Not sick or anything?"

"No."

"What is it?" Scott says. "What was it?"

"What was what?"

"You have something to tell me or something? Why you called me down here. Thought maybe it had to do with Ruth."

Terrell just looks at his feet, then sneaks a glance toward the bridge's wide support, then the river, the bushes. His mouth isn't still, but it doesn't look like it's about to form words. Scott turns and looks behind himself; the river's surface is ridged by the breeze, currents bending the straight lines.

"What?" he says, facing Terrell again. "You're acting a little spooky. You want some advice or something?"

"That's what it is," Terrell suddenly says, and steps closer. "Advice." He grabs hold of Scott, throws an arm around his neck, the other fist swinging at the same time.

The punch catches Scott in the top of the head and he pulls himself free from the headlock, stumbles ten feet away with his hands up, careful not to turn his back.

"What are you thinking?" He stands with one foot in front, his body turned sideways, a kind of martial arts pose. Fingers splayed, palms out, he holds his left hand low, his right hand behind his head. Terrell just stands there; his hands are at his sides, balled into fists, like he doesn't know what to do.

"Don't," Scott says. "I don't want to mess you up." This is true; he doesn't want to hurt Terrell. They're the same size, but that's no excuse, and then there's Ruth. He steals a look behind him, then at the tops of the cars as they slide along the bridge, overhead. He's about to speak again when Terrell raises his hand and takes a step forward, swinging his arm as if he could reach, strike him from ten feet away.

The stone catches Scott right in the sternum, with a crack, almost knocking him down. He turns to run, but before he's taken five steps his legs are gone, tripped away. His arms are caught in the straps of his pack and he can't free them to catch himself. He lands hard on his chest, air huffing out all at once, glasses flying off and eyes closed just before his face slaps into the gravel.

The blows start slowly, then multiply. His legs, his ribs, his head, which he tries to cover with his arms. At first he believes it only feels like more than one person; after a moment, he knows better. Voices roll above, distant people shouting to save him or worse; closer, the voices are high-pitched, half whispering, almost out of breath with beating him. Boys. He tries to tense all his muscles—he's heard something about that—but every kick, every punch still hurts. He keeps his eyes closed.

The blows slow without stopping. He hears the zipper of his pack, laughter as the boys rifle through it, the hollow bounce of his empty water bottle. His hearing gradually tightens, as if he's sinking, his ears filling with liquid. He doesn't raise his head or move at all, for fear the beating will continue. There's no way this isn't happening, right now; for once, his mind won't wander.

Eighteen

Lakeesha's Memory

Y ou're wearing out the wall," the boy says.

Terrell doesn't turn; he keeps throwing the tennis ball against the brick house. The ball bounces differently off the plywood in the one window—the other window's missing, and if he slips, the ball will sail right inside, lost. Terrell is practicing throwing and catching with his left hand, which is not as strong as his right. He feels the three boys behind, watching. They're bigger than he is. This is their neighborhood.

"What's your name, kid?"

"Terrell."

"What're you doing here?"

"Nothing."

"Right. You waiting on someone?"

"No." He almost misses the ball, blocks it with his body. He listens for them to keep walking, and finally they do, their steps fading on the broken glass that shines everywhere, slowly ground back down to sand.

A car rolls by, its stereo blasting. The beat of the bass shivers the row house windows. Terrell feels it on the skin of his arms, in his chest. He's been waiting half an hour and he doesn't know how much longer he can last. A dog barks, unseen down an alley; he remembers what Lakeesha told him about the rottweilers. Her house is close, just down the street. He can't tell if anyone's home, can't decide whether to knock.

Fans prop windows open. Across the street, and above, a man sits in a lawn chair on a fire escape, watching him. The vacant lot is overgrown—long grass sticks through bent shopping carts, wraps around television antennas thrown from rooftops. Something smells rotten, fermented; trash bags are ripped open, garbage cooking in the sun. The boys will be back around soon, circling. Overhead, the shoes dangle from telephone lines. Terrell doesn't want to walk home barefoot.

She cuts in front of him, catches the ball. Somehow he hadn't heard her. She catches it right by her ear, and his empty hand is still out, behind hers. Lakeesha turns, smiling.

"Thought that was you," she says. She wears a white halter top that shows her stomach, the bottom of her sharp rib cage. Her hair's all straightened, pulled back. She throws the ball against the house and he catches it.

"Here to tell me some more about your friend?"

"No," he says.

"Heard about you. Been hearing things."

"How's that?"

"You jumped some homeless guy," she says. "Down by the river."

"Who told you that?"

"I just heard it. Heard he was pretty big."

"I don't know," Terrell says. "He was a man, I guess."

"Crazy."

149

The Ambidextrist

Terrell can't tell whether or not Lakeesha's impressed; the way she smiles, it seems she might be kidding, making fun of him.

"What'd it feel like?" she says.

"All right."

"You going to do it again?"

"It wasn't like I just did it for no reason," Terrell says, throwing the ball. "The man said some things to me. It wasn't the only time I saw him, either. It was lots of little things."

"You're quite the little fighter," she says, and he sees she's not impressed after all.

"Probably won't do it again," he says. "Unless I have to."

"Been waiting long?" she says.

"No, I just did it. I hadn't been thinking about it before."

"I mean have you been here long."

"Not really."

"Didn't know you were coming. Could've called me on the phone."

Now they toss the ball back and forth, softly, five feet between them.

"I'm older than you," she says. "Remember?"

"I know it."

"Maybe I'll call you," she says. "What's your number?"

"Eight seven five, nine three one two."

"What's a good time to call?"

"You won't," he says.

"Why not?"

"You already forgot it."

"I memorized it," she says. "I'll write it down when I get inside. When?"

"At night," he says.

"What if your mom answers?"

"My sister. She won't. She works all night, mostly."

150

"She the only one?"

"What?"

"You live with."

"Yeah."

Lakeesha smiles, tries to trick him by throwing low. "Then I could come right over there," she says. "One night when you're alone. How'd you like that?"

"I don't know," he says.

"I bet you don't." Lakeesha turns and walks away. Halfway to her house, she looks back. She throws the ball, straight to him. "Eight seven five, nine three one two," she says. "I'll call before I come over."

As soon as the door closes, Terrell begins walking. He needs to get out of the neighborhood, and he hopes his head will be clearer, will settle a little bit, once he's farther from Lakeesha.

The idea of her in his house excites and worries him. Would they have enough to talk about? Would they watch TV? Would she laugh at his things? At all the old pictures and everything coming apart? Maybe they would kiss, even do what she had done with Swan. Darnay claimed he'd taken a shower with a girl—maybe they would do that, all their clothes mixed together on the floor, standing next to each other, naked, waiting for the water to get hot.

He heads south on Broad Street, toward City Hall; William Penn stands on top, high above. If Terrell walks fast, it will still take him half an hour to get home. He wonders if Ruth will be there, and whether she's ever taken a shower with someone else. Maybe even with Dwayne, who comes over a lot these days; it's hard to imagine the two of them fitting in the shower at the same time. Maybe Dwayne is there now, even. Terrell doesn't mind him—he puts Ruth in a better mood, and he's not the kind who tries to be Terrell's best friend.

Terrell tries to keep thinking of Lakeesha, of the shower, but his mind keeps slipping back to Scott. He doesn't feel right about what he did, and at the same time he does feel right. It's a relief to have his test done, like the rest of them, and to know that his was the last one except the one they'll all do together. And, he admits to himself, when Scott was down and he was kicking him, there was something he liked about that feeling.

— Nineteen
Electrical Connections

S cott stares into every plate-glass window he passes, every mirror he
can find. Swollen, his right eye hardly opens, and yellow creeps
into the white, shot through with the red of burst blood vessels. Could
he have done anything differently? He doesn't know. He finds it hard
to blame Terrell; he hasn't been able to sort it out in the two days that
have passed. The inside of his mouth's all cut up, from being kicked
into his teeth. He feels each tooth, testing them with his finger. None
are loose. Maybe later today he'll find a barber college, someone who
can feather the sides of his hair right, so they come together in the
back like the tail of a duck. The thought of it makes him feel better.
Hopeful.

It's morning, overcast and hot. As he walks to the hospital, the people he passes turn and look after him; they whisper to each other. His
ribs are blue, black, and green, and his back feels as if it must look the
same way. Working, making money, will help him feel like he's moving

153

forward, he hopes, making progress. He worries that he won't be able to pass the physical for the new trial, that they'll turn him away on appearance alone. Yet when he reaches the hospital, no one comments; they're used to people coming into the lobby looking all sorts of ways.

Even Lisa Roberts hardly glances at him. Together, they rise in the elevator, and then she leads him down hallways, into a small room.

He sits on a padded chair with wheels on its legs; computers surround him, some on desks, some on wheeled carts. The fluorescent hospital lights that always make him sleepy hang above. Outside, in the hallway, stretchers roll and clang, voices blur. Lisa is getting things ready. She wears white running shoes over black tights; her dark skirt hangs halfway between the bend of her knees and her thick ankles. She places a white towel around his shoulders, then points behind him.

"All right?" she says.

"All right," Scott says.

"The larger one will be more comfortable," she says, "but the smaller one will give us a better connection."

What look like two shower caps rest there, fit atop styrofoam heads. White plastic rings the size of Life Savers cover the caps, and thin, colored wires, intertwined, stretch from each one. The tips of the wires are gathered into a many-pronged plug. Lisa lifts the smaller cap. At her first touch, he pulls back a little, then recovers, holds himself steady. Closer, facing him, she takes hold of the cap above each of his ears and jerks it down. One side, then the other, then both at once. He gasps. His skull contracts. His eyes threaten to fall out.

"You're not so talkative today," she says.

"It hurts my face to talk," he says.

"Someone sure got hold of you. I thought you were some kind of karate kid."

"Right. That's me."

"I met someone who knows you," she says. "Another subject. Man named Oliver?"

154

"No," Scott says. "I mean I knew him once, but not anymore. I really don't know him at all."

"I usually don't do this test," she says. "I'm just filling in, today."

"How's your daughter?" he says.

Lisa Roberts stands up straight, stops fitting the cap on his head, and steps back.

"What do you know about my daughter?"

"Just remembered her picture in your office, that's all. And your husband, with those sideburns of his. Man."

"You see that cord," Lisa says, pointing to a gray cable on the wall. "I pull on that and I get orderlies, security, right away. All kinds of people running toward us."

"Whoa," Scott says. "Whoa. Here I am, just passing the time, pleasant and friendly, you know, and you're acting like I'm trying to latch onto you, some way. Come on, now—you and me, we've been through a lot together. You know I'm not like that. You know I'm dependable."

Lisa doesn't answer. She keeps adjusting the cap, pretending she didn't say what she did. Talking nervously, she tells him how the test works, then explains how they can record the electrical activities of the brains of rats and guinea pigs, wires stuck right into their foreheads. Scott listens, thinking he'll never let them put a wire inside him. He's done plenty, though—the magnets, the flashing numbers, the faces—and he'll do more. There's still the sleep studies, or the cameras inside his body, or the stew with tracers in it, where they'd wave the wand over his stomach. He's not afraid, he only wishes she wouldn't compare the experiments to the ones they do on animals.

"This gel's a little cold," Lisa says, taking a tube off a shelf. "But it's a good conductor."

"All aboard," Scott says. He feels the gel on his scalp, straight through his hair. "How long since you done this?"

"Electroencephalography?" she says.

155

That's the only answer she gives. It's hard to move his head, to see what she's doing behind him. The air smells a little like Elmer's glue.

"This isn't dangerous at all?" he says.

"No. Not really."

He sees her take the bundle of wires and plug them into another bundle, which stretches to the computer. The gel is hardening along his scalp, the cap gripping his head even more tightly now. Lisa keeps circling around him, squeezing the tube, making adjustments.

"Well," he says, "since we met, you and me, I've done a lot of moving along since then, started some things developing. Friends, you know—a whole collection of people."

Lisa bends down, looking at his head like a barber would, trying to get the sides even.

"You know," he continues, "it's more than just being familiar with people, too. I got other people's problems I worry about, and they all look after me, too."

"I thought you said talking hurt your face. You're throwing off my adjustment, the way you're moving your mouth."

She shows him the grid of squares on the computer screen across the room; he squints his left eye to make it out. Each square flickers, between yellow and blue and pink. Once they're dark blue, that shows the connection of the electrodes is solid.

"Then what?"

"We get a line in your arm, a tracer in your blood, and we'll wheel you, along with all the computers you're attached to, into that little room there, where you'll do some tests."

"Where I choose whether people's faces are sad or happy or neither?"

"Maybe."

"That gets harder the more you do it."

"I'll be right back," Lisa Roberts says. "We have to wait for the connections to take hold."

Electrical Connections

Left alone, Scott's afraid he'll fall asleep and his neck will slump and his head will hit something, that the cap will come loose. His neck is stiff. He can't stand up with his head anchored like this, can't stretch, can hardly move. He feels a little queasy, the electrodes heavy against his skull, the wires brushing the skin of his neck. Perhaps something is wrong with him, perhaps he's being slowly electrocuted. He thinks of the magnetic fields they'd passed through his brain, and of the magnets he'd been given in grade school, when he was a child; in his mind, thoughts spin and turn toward one another, and memories. Some are attracted and join together; others are pushed away. He wills Lisa Roberts to return. At the drug companies' trials, they'd pay him in full, let him out early, but he had to get really, really sick before that would happen. When he had thrown up, in bathrooms, watched by a monitor with a clipboard, when he was blinded by headaches, when he rocked back and forth on tile floors with his stomach twisted cold—all those times, he told himself he was feeling that way so others wouldn't have to.

"Almost there," Lisa says. He hadn't heard her footsteps. "Perfect," she says, pointing to the computer screen.

All the squares are deep purple. Scott is proud to see it. He decides not to say anything about his uneasiness, the pulses in his head, to see if he can make it through without stopping the test.

"Happy, sad, neutral," he says. "I'm ready."

"A few more electrodes. I'll try to be gentle around the eye, here."

"I got electricity in my face?"

"Oh, yes." Lisa sticks her fingertip in a small glass jar. "A little glue." He feels it, cold, her finger pressing at his forehead, then his temple, then below his eye. The electrodes, round and metal, with wires like legs, come next.

He loses control of his left eye. It blinks, then again.

"Whoa," he says.

"What is it?"

157

It comes in pulses. He wants to pull it all off his face, but he's afraid to wreck the test, to undo all the work. Then the pain comes around again—his eye rolls, beyond his control, like someone's inside his skull, poking the walls with a sharp stick. He cries out. His eyelid is wild, snapping, dry.

Lisa Roberts saves him. She pulls off the wires, the electrodes. She hits the switch. Her hand is on his face.

"It's just not supposed to do that," she says. "It shouldn't be possible."

"It did," Scott says. "It is."

Pulling out a chair from somewhere behind him, she sets it close. She sits down and it totters, one leg is too short. She looks as shaky as he feels.

"Let's try it again," he says.

"It'll just shock you again."

"It might not."

"It will."

"That's all right."

"No, it's not all right."

Standing, Lisa takes hold of the cap on each side, just above his ears. She pulls, almost jerking him from his chair. The cap comes off with a pop.

Scott reaches up and feels his head, his hair dried into sticky ridges.

"We've got a sink where you can rinse that out," Lisa says. She stares at the screen, upset, all the squares going yellow and red. Her voice is lower. "It'll take the rest of the day to figure this out, explain it."

"But you didn't learn anything at all from that," Scott says. "You want help? I could do something."

"You'll still get paid," she says, "if that's what you're wondering."

"It wasn't."

Reaching down, Scott slides his backpack along the floor. He unzips the pocket, then unfolds the black plastic eyeglasses.

"Here," he says.

Lisa takes the glasses, hardly looking at them; she sets them on a shelf.

"Didn't mean to take them," he says. "No one asked for them. Later, I realized I'd walked off with them, so I brought them back."

Lisa is looking at the empty cap, folded on the floor, snarled with wires. She touches it with the toe of her white shoe.

Scott had expected more. Surprise, or gratitude. He stands. On the way out, he considers trying to slip the glasses back into his pack, but he does not. The halls stretch, blurry around him, as he walks away, heading for the elevator.

Twenty
Negotiations

R uth sees him coming, all the way down the terminal. He rocks up
and down in his cowboy boots, gaining a couple inches of height
with one step, losing it with the next. His smile is visible at fifty feet,
completely phony.

She stands next to the scanner, waiting. His hair is wet, a part
straight up the middle, each side swept back. He stands, not saying a
word. A bleached white circle marks the front of his red polo shirt,
which is too small. The skin of his neck and jaw is discolored, yellows
and blues just beneath the surface; he has fresh cuts under his chin, in
front of his ear.

"Just shave?" she says.

"You've always got hot water here. Mine's out, where I been living." He pauses. Up close, his smile looks painful, pathetic. "Lots of
people shave in the rest rooms, you know."

"New glasses?"

Negotiations

The frames are gold, teardrop shaped. The lenses are the kind that change with light, and they're caught halfway, so his eyes are only partially visible, staring out through a haze.

"My own prescription," he says. "They made these in under an hour."

"So what is it now?" she says.

"How's that? The time?"

"What is it you want from me?"

"Lunch," he says. "I want to take you to lunch."

"Right," she says.

"I got money, if that's what you're wondering."

"You must, coming to the airport to buy lunch." She reaches behind her, lifting her square, leather bag. "I bring my own," she says, "but I'll eat it with you."

"You're serious?"

"Don't act so surprised," she says. "I've been waiting for you. We have some things to talk about."

"Right on," Scott says, following her.

His boots clock along, while Ruth's service oxfords are silent. People pull luggage on wheels; suitcases tail around corners, tip onto their sides. Above, a recorded voice circles, warning about leaving cars parked at the terminal curbside, about leaving one's baggage unattended. Scott waits for the message to finish, for the space before it starts again, and then he speaks.

"I like your hair," he says. "Those braids and everything."

Ruth just smiles, nods. They both know it's an obvious thing to say.

"Where you want to eat?" she says. "Kenny Rogers?"

"What about him?" Scott says, and then he turns and sees the restaurant. He stares at the people inside, the cashiers in their uniforms, the picture of the man with the light gray hair and beard. He closes his eyes, opens them again.

"What's the matter?" Ruth says.

"I don't think I can eat in there."

"Can't or won't?"

"Both," he says.

Ruth laughs. "What do you feel like eating?"

"Pancakes."

"Pancakes," she says. "Follow me." She points farther down the terminal.

Out on the tarmac, planes wheel slowly around, just missing each other. The ground crews scramble under the wings, wearing orange vests, shorts, and kneepads, headphones over their ears. Above it all, the tower stands, and all the radar, invisible in the air. Scott stays close to Ruth as they move through the crowd.

"Thing of it is," he says. "I know Kenny Rogers. I worked for him."

"At the restaurant?"

"Someone must have tricked him," Scott says. "Or he had some money problems or something. I saw plenty, you know. Saw him sing 'Islands in the Stream' with Dolly Parton where I could have reached out and touched her."

"Who's this?"

"Kenny Rogers," Scott says.

"He was a singer?" Ruth says. "I thought he was just a chicken guy, like Colonel Sanders."

"He is a singer. Not 'was.' "

"Here," Ruth says, slowing. "This isn't the cheapest, but I don't know where else you're getting pancakes this late in the day."

They pass through an entryway of cheap stained glass. It's a cocktail lounge with a restaurant attached; the lights are dimmer than in the terminal, and faint music plays, overwhelmed by the televisions above the bar. Three different baseball games are on, the grass in each diamond a different shade of green. Scott follows Ruth. Over in the smoking section, a gray haze settles five feet off the floor.

Negotiations

They sit in a booth, facing each other. She checks the watch on her wrist.

"Have to get back?" he says, noticing.

"No," she says. "We're going to talk some things out."

"I like the sound of that," he says.

The waitress pours them each a cup of coffee, then leaves the insulated pitcher on the table.

"Stack of pancakes," Scott says. "Buttermilk."

"I'm good with the coffee," Ruth says.

The waitress looks like she might say something about Ruth bringing in her own food, then sees the uniform, the badge sewn on the blazer, and thinks better of it. Ruth takes out a bag of carrot sticks and points with one before snapping it in her teeth.

"Take off the glasses," she says. "I want to see your eyes while I'm talking to you."

Scott takes off his glasses. His small eyes, surrounded by bruises, blink at her. His hair is almost dry, one side sticking up above a cowlick. She can hardly find the anger in her, looking at him.

"One thing I'm trying to understand," she says. "Is why we keep coming together."

"Fate?" he says.

"No, it's definitely not fate. What it is, is one of us must be making it happen. And I'm pretty sure I'm not the one."

"Fair enough," Scott says.

"It made me angry," she says. "At first. Now I'm over that."

"Good."

"Not that it couldn't come back. Now, though, I'm curious. What is it? Me? My little brother? I don't know."

"I'm not sure this is going the way I wanted it to go," he says.

"That's right." Ruth reaches into her bag and pulls out a piece of paper. She sets it faceup on the table. It's the MRI image of his head, taken from the side, showing all the twists of his brain.

"Found this in my house," she says. "Terrell's room. Know anything about how it got there?"

"No," Scott says. "I lost it."

"I don't believe that—you were so proud of it."

"It got old, after a while."

"I want you to talk to me, here. Did you give it to him? Did he take it?" She sips at her coffee, trying to calm her rising impatience.

"He must have found it," Scott says. "I guess."

"And what about you and Terrell? What's going on there? You saying you're friends and everything."

"Nothing," he says, setting down his fork for a moment, playing with his glasses. "I just know his name—that's about it."

"And what happened to your face?" she says.

"Thought you hadn't noticed."

"Who did it?"

"Doesn't matter," he says, unfolding his napkin. "Listen, he's a smart kid, Terrell is. But you get a group of smart ones together and they go beyond stupid. The stupidity multiplies. You got to watch that—I do what I can, but here pretty soon I'll be doing some work in the hospital where it won't be real easy for me to get out, keep anything from happening."

"Now you're talking like it's more than just knowing his name."

"Listen, Ruth—"

"Don't even start," she says. "Am I supposed to lock him in? Worry more than I do already? And why should I be listening to you? Do I want him to live like you?"

"Whoa," Scott says, his palms up, flashing at her. "I'm not saying he pisses sitting down—nothing like that."

"I don't know what it is," she says. "I just want you to stay away from him. I want you to promise me."

"That goes both ways," he says. "You know that. I can try to stay out of his way, but he comes looking for me, what am I supposed to do? You know I just want to help him."

"I don't know that. Not at all."

Scott looks away, pretending to study the painting next to him, of a horse race—twenty horses, the jockeys on their backs wearing all different colors. Before Ruth can speak again, the waitress returns, setting a plate on the table.

"Decent stack of pancakes can really stay with you, over the course of a day." Scott sets to work, cutting the stack all one way, then the other, at right angles. "This way's more efficient—gets your appetite going, and the syrup gets down into the whole stack." He takes his first bite of the pancakes, then spreads the butter with his fork, then takes another bite. He doesn't pause until half the plate is clean.

"I can't believe you never listened to Kenny Rogers," he says, pushing the crumbs into a pool of syrup, licking his finger. "You never heard 'Lady'? Or 'Don't Fall in Love with a Dreamer'? How about 'You Decorated My Life'?"

"You ever see any black folks at his shows?" Ruth says.

"I don't know. Can't remember. That's a real good point, though."

"My break's over," Ruth says, standing. She lays two dollar bills on the table.

"No way," Scott says, handing them back to her. "My treat. That was the deal. I could've afforded a lot more, too. Could've had sausages on the side, anything."

"I want you to stay away from Terrell."

"You're leaving this for me, right?" He holds up the paper, the picture of his brain.

"Did you hear what I said? About Terrell?"

"How about except under your supervision?" he says. "Like if we were all together? Because this lunch, here, I think it's a productive step. I can see you're warming to me."

165

"Unbelievable," Ruth says. "All right. Just stay away from him unless I'm there, too. How's that?"

"Perfect," Scott says. "I can see the three of us already."

She walks away, uncertain of what she's accomplished. Looking back, she sees Scott taking a handful of change from his pack. He counts out the coins, concentrating, stacking them in quarters, dimes, and nickels.

Twenty-one

Machinery

The phone rings in the kitchen, and there she is, right in Terrell's ear. Lakeesha.

"Tonight," she says. "I might come on over there, see what you're doing."

"Not tonight," he says. "I can't."

"Maybe I'll track your friend Swan down," she says. "He lives by me. Closer."

"He won't be home," Terrell says. "And he doesn't want to talk to you, anyway."

"Where the two of you going?"

"I'll tell you later, if I can."

"Maybe," she says. "Maybe not."

An hour later, he has almost forgotten her. The boys walk four abreast, as if they hold a rope between them, or are tied together. It's dark along the river, the water flat and heavy looking, black as oil. A

167

tree trunk floats close to the bank, its rough bark like the back of an alligator in the moonlight.

They walk. Darnay pulls ahead, then falls back in step; Swan rises, taller as he steps on the greasy wood of the railroad ties. He's looking ahead, over at the river. He doesn't seem to be thinking of Lakeesha; it's been a long time since he's even mentioned her name.

"So what are we trying to do?" John says.

"We don't know that yet," Terrell says.

Downriver, the windows of tall buildings shine. The half moon is yellow, bright. Atop the Peco Building, lighted words circle, BACK TO SCHOOL 11:47.

"Think we should know what we're doing?" Darnay says.

"We'll find out," Swan says.

"Stupid question like that's why we started the tests," John says, and they all laugh since he asked the question in the first place. They're all easier with each other, looser. It's no one's test tonight—it's everyone's. They slow, approaching the trees, then pick up the pace when they're under them. As they pass through the shadows, their white shoes are all that's visible.

It feels different here than in the daytime, or the same as it usually does, only more. A couple of cars are parked, idling, up by Vine Street—men coming to buy, smoke, or find a date for the night. Leaves slither against each other, rustled by the wind or unseen people. Voices murmur from the bushes. The boys are closer together, quieter. They don't want to draw more attention than they have already.

They go down, under the overpass, nearer the river. Flames glow above, on the right, where people stand smoking at the top of the concrete slope, their heads almost touching the underside of the bridge. They stay there; they do not descend. The boys pass through, out the other side.

A chain-link fence circles the waterworks, razor wire across the top.

Machinery

The engine house stands like a forgotten church, all the smaller structures lined along the river, clustered close. The pillars glow faintly beneath the moon; they hold all the shadows behind them, as if the darkness might spill out. Construction trailers and machinery wait for the morning, when everything will be put into motion. Across the river, headlights blink and sweep away. The boys stand silently, taking it in.

It's John who speaks: "We could cut the fence, just a straight line." He catches himself, before one of the others says it—" 'Course, we got nothing to cut it with."

Terrell kneels and pulls at the fence; a clip, holding it to the nearest post, pops off. Down on his stomach, crawling along, he feels a scratch at the back of his neck, his leg, and then he's clear. The fence pulls back, raking the dirt when he lets go.

Sometimes, in alleys, in vacant lots, security lights snap on, triggered by motion sensors. There's nothing like that here. Standing, Terrell squints. Something's about to happen. He walks away from the fence; each step brings new shapes from the shadows, shows their outlines against the moonlit sky. A bulldozer, then a taller machine, with a bent metal tail hooked out behind it. Terrell hears the others, the rattle of the fence. He passes close to a trailer. GOLDBERG ELECTRICAL, the sign says.

He runs ahead, toward the engine house, around a cement mixer. Plywood covers the window and he pulls at the edge, bowing it out. Splinters dig into his hand as he squeezes through. The plywood slaps shut.

He slides his feet sideways a little, moving out of the way for whoever's behind him. It's so dark that he's afraid to take a step; he could fall off a ledge, into a hole. He holds a hand in front of his face, so he won't put out an eye.

Overhead, wings slap the black air. Moonlight lines the edges of the boards across the windows. That's all. Terrell doesn't hear any voices, any footsteps behind him, anyone following. He holds his breath, and thinks he hears breathing, rustling. Very close, though it's hard to say. Then the words, seeming to come from both sides at once.

"I knew you'd come." A man's voice. "I've been waiting."

"What?" Terrell says. He steps away from the narrow line of light at the window, so he'll be harder to see. He hopes he's moving farther from the voice.

"Come closer."

"You stay where you are," Terrell says.

"Easy. Maybe you can't tell who I am. Do you know? My name is Ray. I'm your friend. All you boys. What's your name?"

Terrell doesn't speak. He holds his breath, unable to tell if the old man is getting closer, crawling toward him. Now he knows who the man is—the same one who follows them on his bicycle, watching while they splash in fountains, who appears everywhere they go. Where are the others now? Terrell knows this would count for the final test—the four of them here, with the old man in the dark. They could do whatever they wanted, and they'd even talked about it, about getting him. Now, though, Terrell wants to get away. He tries to feel the wall behind him, tries to find the edge of the window.

"Yes, I knew you'd come," the man says, closer now.

"No," Terrell says. He steps back into the window, the plywood against his cheek. Twisting himself away, he struggles outside again. He expects a hand to take hold of his foot, to hear the sound of the plywood pushed out again. He shivers, looks back. The man isn't following. Not yet.

Lights spill from the windows of one trailer. Closer, he sees his friends inside, their three backlit heads, their skinny arms pointing at each other. He runs toward them, around the other side. DELUCA CONSTRUCTION, the sign says. He goes up the wooden steps, the door wide open.

As he enters, the three look up, startled, trying to find something to hide behind. They all wear yellow hard hats, too big, wobbling on their heads.

"Where you been?"

"You broke the lock?"

"Door was open."

The trailer is cramped; there's not much room for all four of them to stand. Blueprints cover tilted desks; other drawings hang on the wall. John and Swan are smoking—a pack of cigarettes lies open on a bench. Darnay holds a book of matches.

"Wonder how all this would burn?" he says. He picks up a black plastic radio, splattered with paint, and drops it on the floor; it bounces once, the antenna clattering loose.

"Got to turn out the lights," Terrell says. "Everyone can see us through the windows, see we're in here from a long way away."

"There's no one here."

"Could be, pretty fast."

John's holding a metal flashlight as long as his arm. He hits the light switch. It's dark, and then the beam zigzags across the floor, along the walls.

"Let's just tear it all up," Darnay says. The light is on his face, then gone; he doesn't look tired at all, as if it's the middle of the day.

"Let's go in the buildings," Swan says.

"There's nothing in there," Terrell says.

The yellow beam of light jerks from face to face, spins along the walls, the ceiling, then stops, doubles back.

"Keys," John says. He steps toward them, the flashlight beam going sharper and brighter, shrinking down on the nail where the keys hang. He holds them in his hand and the other boys cluster around. There are three keys, a masking tape tag on each one. FORKLIE, CATTER, TRACTO.

"You got here last, Terrell," John says. He hands Swan and Darnay each a key.

171

As Terrell turns, he sees a line of tiny red lights, glowing in a corner. "Hold on," he says.

It's six walkie-talkies, charging their batteries. They're heavy, black, with short, rigid antennas. Each boy takes one.

"Switch it on. Put it on 'A.'"

"Hello," Swan says. "This working?"

"Can't tell. We're too close."

"Let's go," Darnay says, holding his key in the light.

They jump down the steps, back outside, toward the machines. Swan's hard hat falls, bounces; he does not slow to pick it up, and the hollow sound echoes, settles. Terrell runs after Swan, climbing up onto the bulldozer, crouched on the metal plates of its tread.

"This starts, you'll get pulled right under," Swan says. He sits in the ripped black seat, foam rubber showing through. He tries to fit the key.

Terrell looks over and sees John in the forklift. Darnay's in the big tractor, but the bulldozer's blade makes him hard to see. The tractor's lights suddenly bolt out, the engine catches, rumbles. The whole hulking thing lurches forward, five feet, then dies, the lights closing down.

Swan turns the key and there's only a clicking.

"That mean it's dead? Think you have to do something else?"

"I don't know."

The air is hot in Terrell's throat; it tastes like coal, like something is burning. The chain-link fence glows, stretching all around, and everything inside is coming alive. He wonders if they'll ram each other, if they'll plow into the buildings. He's ready to see it.

Now Darnay's got the tractor going, and Terrell jumps down, runs toward it. The back tire's turning, almost as tall as he is, and he leaps in front of it, onto the running board, the step below where Darnay is sitting, the wheel in both hands, the walkie-talkie vibrating along the dash. They hunch down a slope, onto the bricks. Terrell sees John has the forklift going—he runs it right into the trailer, crumpling one cor-

172

ner, the whole thing slipping from its cinder blocks and landing at an angle.

The arm on the back of the tractor goes ten feet up, then elbows down, its end a square-toothed shovel, big enough to hold a person. The shovel drags behind them, bouncing, and the headlights open everything up, clearing shadows from every corner, reflecting in the broken black windows. Terrell's left hand grips Darnay's seat, his right on a handhold along the fender; his feet bounce, but do not come off. The heat from the engine slices around him. The shovel rattles, bouncing out sparks in their wake.

Swan suddenly appears from one side, into the lights and running all the way across, the walkie-talkie still in his hand as he zigzags back, hands above his head, turning to squint at them, running ahead again.

They can't keep this up—it's too loud, they'll be caught—but it's impossible to stop, not to stretch it a little farther. Darnay shouts something and Terrell shouts back; they can't understand a word, and it doesn't matter. Off a step and still going, the engine revs higher, whining, and Darnay doesn't know how to shift. They sideswipe a pillar and the tire just bounces off, shifting their direction. Nothing falls from above. Everything barely holds. They head onto the open stretch, the balustrade ticking by on the left, trading shadows among its spokes, the dark river below, and the sky above, the headlights cutting a bright swath between them.

Swan darts into the light again, so close, dancing. Darnay turns the wheel to follow.

Just a little more light might make it easier; then again, that might make it impossible. And everything seems possible now. Ray is flat on his stomach, trying to get closer. If he could only reach a little farther along the floor, he'd have hold of the ankle, just hold the boy to con-

vince him to sit down. Hardly a touch, barely cheating. That's all he
wants. No one ever understands that, but the boys have. All the work
he's done for them. They understand him. They've heard his calls.

"Yes, I knew you'd come," he says. The cardboard beneath him
slides along the grit next to his ear, obscuring the boy's answer. Now he
sees the shape of the slim body, backlit against the window, slipping
outside again.

Ray feels the weight of his own body, the dull pain resting on his
hip, shoulder blade, the side of his head. Standing, he stretches. His
joints crack, ligaments strain, and then it all settles, winds itself, ready.
He'll wait. They know where he is. The boy had said he'd be right
back, or something like it, and he'll return with the others. Ray can no
longer hear them. Should he follow? He stands still, darkness around
him. What a fortunate night it is, all the hours left. The boys will be
back—they've come this far. Was there room on the cardboard for all
of them? They might stay up all night, shoulder to shoulder, talking,
telling ghost stories. In the morning he'll show them the garden, everything. He has so much to tell them he can hardly stand it.

He hears the engines; it takes a moment to make sense of it. The
machinery. That will slow the boys' return, but it means they haven't
left him. He hears their high-pitched shouting, their laughter, and he
wants to join them, wants them to hurry.

He's waited this long. He is ready. He'll fix a bicycle for each of
them, show them what he knows. Teach them to swim. Tell them
about when he was a boy himself, back in Delaware. The story of the
snapping turtle and all the other stories, the ones he's read. They had
heard his calling! And there's still some summer left. He'll show them.

Suddenly, the engines go silent, muffled. There's a heavy buckling
crash, a deep concussion that jolts his knees. He does not fall. The
voices are like women screaming. They fade. The whole foundation
shakes, eases; he closes his eyes against the grit raining from the rafters.
This is not right. He steps toward the window.

Machinery

Outside, in the moonlight, the forklift is still running. Its tires slip as it pushes against the fence, pulling metal posts loose as it attempts to drag the whole thing away, a stiff net behind it. Down past the pillars, what he sees is stranger still. He jerks closer, lifting his feet.

Where the bricks give way to asphalt, a crater has opened. Light and smoke sift up from it, dissipating. Ray makes it through the pillars, breathing hard. He slows, afraid to get too close to the hole, the edge crumbling away. Holding his breath, he tries to step lightly. The abandoned swimming pool is thirty feet below, dry, the yellow tractor settled in the middle of it. The tractor's one headlight is still shining, the engine still running, chortling smoke. Ray leans closer and then he sees the boy, spread out to one side, all the way down there, not moving.

"Hello?" Ray shouts. There's no answer, not from any direction.

Turning, he heads back the way he came. His knees jerk his feet ahead; he cannot feel the ground. Back in the engine house, he moves by touch, along the walls, between the metal frames of the new scaffolding. He finds the smooth inlet hole, where water once passed—he can hear it in his ears, like the inside of a shell—and he folds himself in, crawls through, into a tunnel, underground passages no one else knows, no one remembers.

The darkness smells of fish, of dirt. Blood pulses in his ears, yet he follows the sound of the engine, the faint light ahead. He emerges into the huge room, the cavern that holds the swimming pool.

The machine has landed on its side, smashed straight through the bottom of the pool, into the dirt. The upper wheel turns, slapping the shreds of its tire. The headlight still shines, reflecting off broken tiles; the walls flicker, spray paint spelling words he cannot read.

Dropping into the pool, he collapses to his knees, cuts his palms on the shards of tiles. He crawls to the boy, reaches out to gently touch his shoulder. He presses his ear to the boy's back, but can hear nothing over the engine. He considers turning the body over, but he hesitates.

175

He whispers to the boy, to himself. He stares up through the jagged hole, at the pale stars in the sky.

And then the engine sputters and dies, the wheel slows; the head-light dims, yet holds. It's so quiet Ray expects an explosion at any moment. The boy's breathing is jagged, speeding up, slowing down, catching again. One leg twitches of its own accord. The water slithers, echoing, the river close on the other side of the wall. The explosion doesn't come.

Ray struggles to lift him, to get the boy over his shoulder. Turning a slow circle, he can see no others, no one else. He staggers toward the pool's edge, sliding his feet, kicking sharp tiles loose. If they can make it to the garden, everything will work out; it might take time to heal him, but they will have that time, if they can get through this. The boy is pressed against him, still breathing, or perhaps that's Ray's own breathing, his lungs filling and collapsing enough for both of them. He moves as if the pool is still full of water, chest deep, and he must force his way through.

The corroded ladder breaks off in his hand. He drops it, clattering around his feet. As he does so, new light fills the cave, white, shining from above. Sirens and red lights whip across the opening, filter down. Squinting, leaning back, he tries to understand the voices shouting, the faces hidden behind all that brightness.

Twenty-two
Early-Morning Hours

The clock on the mantel is ticking, spinning its hands. Ruth is about to throw it out the window. She's still in her security uniform, her tie unclipped, her shoelaces loosened. It's after five in the morning—she knows that without being reminded.

Dwayne sits facing her, in her father's old easy chair. A history of the Civil War rests, closed, in his lap. He drove over from West Philly at three, without any question. She appreciates that he hasn't asked for an explanation, and the way his calm eyes take in the room—never quite settling, yet never staring. He wears a striped pajama shirt, rubber sandals, and doesn't even look tired, though he must be. She must be, too. She can't tell.

They pretend not to notice the sirens; she listens to every one with dread, with hope. The clock ticks. The sirens fade. The windows are wide open, but there's no breeze. Flies find their way through the patched screens, bounce along the walls.

177

Standing, Dwayne crosses the room. He sits next to Ruth on the couch and the springs give way, drawing her toward him. He takes hold of her hand.

"How late is he usually out?"

"I have no idea. Not this late. You know the hours I work."

"Think we should call the police?"

"That's bad luck," Ruth says. "If you do it before sunrise, it is."

"Want to go looking?"

She shakes her head. She's afraid Dwayne will keep talking, try to start a conversation, but he does not. The room is silent except for the flies. The lamps glow and shine through their shades, casting round circles of light onto the cracked ceiling. The clock sounds the half hour.

Twenty-three

Buried Alive

t is a county fair, in Ray's dream, all the stands and stalls set up in the morning, ready by afternoon. Rides, animals, games of chance and skill. He sneaks in early, taking a back way, through a stand of trees. Clouds slip between the branches overhead, and then he's out from under and the sky is wide open. No one notices. It's as if he's invisible as he moves around the metal pieces of the Tilt-A-Whirl, as he runs his fingers along the canvas sides of tents. In one tent, games are being set up for children. A whole room is four feet deep in small plastic balls of every color. Checking around him, certain no one is watching, he burrows himself into the balls, under them, until he's completely hidden. He tries not to breathe too deeply, to get by on what air sifts through. It smells of plastic. Struggling, he rolls over, so he rests on his back, and he lies there, motionless, careful so the surface of the balls will not tremble and betray him. He sleeps. Later, he's awakened by the gentle pressure as the children move around him, lunging and swimming

179

through the plastic balls. Their voices, laughter, sound above, filter down. He lies still, hardly breathing. It is only a matter of time before one of them touches him.

When he is awakened, it is by voices, by laughter. And he is underground, though no one will tell him exactly where. It's a police station, not far from the museum and the waterworks. These are only holding cells, not a true jail. It was the day before this one that they brought him in, led him down the stairs, started in with the fingerprints, the questions, trying to find out who he is.

"Everyone has a last name," they tell him.

The air smells like sweat, dried and thawed out again. The men in the other cells shout back and forth; card games, people they know in common, future plans. There is no future here, hardly any past—it's a constant present, every time the same. Ray needs to get out. This is like a shelter, and worse; he's unable to move, and they feed him on their schedule, whatever they want. His cell is the one they keep for crazies—there's clear plastic just outside the bars, so he won't spit, throw shit, or piss. He can hardly breathe, exhaling the same stale air, taking it back in. Perhaps they're trying to humiliate him, or keep him separate from the other prisoners. He doesn't care.

The sergeant of these underground cells is a smooth black guy, not much younger than Ray. He wears a shirt and tie, not a uniform, and he smokes, offers cigarettes only to deny them.

"Part of why you're in here is to make you a little uncomfortable, you know, where you can't do those things you're used to being able to do. That might help you reflect on how you came to be here, you know?"

That's how it is, hour after hour, cigarette smoke drifting in, cigarettes Ray can't have. Twice, officers have come for him, led him up the stairs for more questions.

"Now the boy couldn't have done all that by himself," the detective says. "Started up all that heavy machinery."

"Maybe he wasn't alone," Ray says.

"What makes you say that?"

"A guess. That's all."

This detective never even pretends to be his friend, doesn't even bother to act sympathetic. He's already hinted that Ray threw the boy into the pool, that the police arrived just as he was hiding the body, the evidence of what he'd done. When Ray says he doesn't know what happened, that he only got there after the fact, the detective says that all criminals say so, that they've never done anything wrong.

"Does that mean it's the innocent who always confess?" Ray says.

"Don't get smart with me. Isn't there something you want to tell me? Something you've forgotten?"

"This just happened. Haven't had time to forget it."

"You know what might happen in a prison population, when they find out what you're in for, what kind of person you are?"

"What kind?" he says. "The kind that tries to help a hurt boy?"

"No reason to get worked up."

"I got every reason."

"No one knows you're in here."

"Tell me about the boy," Ray says.

"You know him, then!"

"Just asking if he pulled through. That's a natural thing to ask."

"You know," the detective tells him, "the boy has friends. And they know you. They've told us about you."

A whole life spent learning how to slip away, to blend in and disappear, has ended like this. Now they have hold of him. He thinks of his bicycle, in its night hiding place. If he's still locked up when the leaves fall from the trees, someone will find it. Maybe before then. He'll need the bicycle, if he ever gets out.

Closing his eyes, he tries to remember his dream, all the colored balls, the smell of plastic, the children so close. He wishes he could sleep, dream all the time; awake, he never feels at home, since he's seen these other places, glimpses of them. The comparison is why he built the garden, to try to get the world to measure up. He wanted the boys to hear that, to see it, to know it. He imagines the garden—all the wooden animals gathered around, the reflecting pool catching light and shadow, no sound except his own breathing, the birds above.

"Mr. Ray."

Cigarette smoke drifts in. Ray waits a moment before opening his eyes. The sergeant leans close, his face cut by the bars, breath fogging the clear plastic.

"The boy is dead," he says. "Passed an hour ago."

— Twenty-four
— Awake

Scott has been locked inside the hospital for sixty-nine hours; another three and they'll let him leave. This is a sleep-deprivation experiment, yet he does not want to sleep. He wants to walk around outside, breathe some fresh air. Wired, far beyond thoughts of rest, he waits, lets the clock wind tighter. His eyes blink faster than usual, his knee bounces almost imperceptibly, his hands will not be still. Waves of prickly heat creep across his skin, under his clothes. This day has no end.

Electrodes are glued to his chin, along his hairline, at his wrist, atop his head. Wires hang down his back, hooked into a monitor he pushes wherever he goes. Every hour and a half he does tests—the colors, the happy and sad faces, the shopping-list memorization, the personality inventories—and then has an hour and a half when he can do anything he wants. Anything except leave, sleep, exercise, or shower.

The Ambidextrist

Everyone's too cheerful, pretending to be sympathetic. They ask him the same questions, hours apart, to see if he changes or can even remember his answers. All the food they give him tastes like metal; he suspects it might not be real, though he doesn't voice this suspicion.

In experiments like this one, they always pair off the subjects, so one monitor can watch the two, and so they'll watch each other. The monitors are partly there to be certain the subjects don't fall asleep, and partly to observe and take notes. The monitors rotate; today they have Lisa Roberts, who wears her clean white coat, looking as if she's just awakened from a solid eight hours.

Scott slides his boots along the linoleum. Overhead, it's the same stained acoustic tiles. That never changes. And the hours are longer, heavier, because he's been paired with his old acquaintance, Oliver, whom he's successfully avoided for over a month.

"I've seen worse," Oliver says. "Done plenty harder."

Scott doesn't listen, he just imagines himself in other places, dreaming with his eyes open. He tries to think of Ruth, but mostly it's Ray who fills his thoughts—he imagines himself and Ray in the garden, under the sound of the green leaves in the wind overhead. They will roll up their pant legs and soak their feet in the cool water of the pond; they'll laugh together and then sit silently, not worrying who will speak next.

Oliver's keeping a monologue going, pausing to give Scott a chance to contribute, then taking off in another direction. He sits nearby, a box for syringe disposal above his head; a sign shows a huge syringe, bright red, and a long thin needle. Oliver still wears his tweed vest, sandals on his sockless feet. His toes are dirty.

"Some sleep trials go on for weeks," he says; the wires attached to him quiver as he talks. He has a new reddish mustache that gets caught between his thin lips. Burst blood vessels have spread from his nose across his cheeks. It's been twenty hours since Scott has spoken to

Oliver, and this is no doubt very interesting to Lisa Roberts, who writes on her clipboard. Times are listed down the left margin.

"I been in those trials," Oliver is saying. "Some, they keep a rectal probe in to register your temperature, and they're drawing blood every half hour. This is nothing. Remember all that, Scotty? Hell, sometimes they just wake you up whenever you start to dream—no REM, you know, and even me or you could go psychotic." He snaps his fingers to show how fast. "Rats," he says, "rats die after being deprived of sleep for seventeen days, you know that? Wires shock them if they try to sleep. They eat more and more, and still they lose weight. Their skin goes bad and then they die."

"Are you two feeling irritable?" Lisa Roberts says, her pen ready to begin writing again, hovering there.

"He is a little irritable," Oliver says. "I certainly think he is. What's the matter, Scotty? You sleepy or something?"

"I been up this long when I wasn't even getting paid." Scott's trying to watch the television, a game show that's beyond impossible to understand. He turns away, his eyes passing over the colors of magazines, fanned across a table. The newspaper's headline is bigger, darker than anything else:

BOY DEAD IN WATERWORKS INCIDENT
VAGRANT SUSPECT IN CUSTODY

He can hardly hold it steady enough to read it. They have no photograph of Ray, the police withheld the mug shot, but the drawing looks just enough like him to be recognizable—the white beard, the smooth Afro, his eyes set back and looking out. There's an outcry; people want him punished. The article doesn't name the boy, that's the family's wish, but it does say three of his friends have come forward, provided information. That makes perfect sense.

185

"What day is it?" Scott says to Lisa.

"Tuesday," she says.

"The number, I mean. The date."

"August fifteenth."

It's yesterday's paper, and no doubt plenty has happened since then, while he's been locked in the hospital, wide awake. This all makes sense to him. He sees exactly what's happened. Sometimes it's not enough to just warn someone, and now they'll do what they want with Ray, turn the story around when the old man has no friend to stand up for him. Scott feels the electricity going, popping just beneath his skull. There's a lot to do, no sleep in sight, and he'll do it or he'll burn down trying.

Standing, he jerks at the wires so the electrodes pop loose from his chin and face and wrists; they swing, rattling against the monitor as he unplugs himself.

"He's bugging!" Oliver says, clapping his hands. "Two hours left and he's falling right off his high horse!"

Scott's already in the hallway, Lisa Roberts close behind him.

"Wait," she says.

"I have to go." He holds up the newspaper. "I got a friend in trouble."

"Just one more test," she says. "You've been such an exemplary subject."

The heels of his boots echo down the white hallway.

Scott walks toward the police station, checking himself in the windows he passes. On the way from the hospital, he bought a new shirt at the Salvation Army—Western, with fake-pearl snaps for buttons—and a pair of black polyester pants with sharp creases flaring out over his scuffed boots. He had to do it. He's even sacrificed his hair, sat down in the barber's chair and asked for the same haircut all the businessmen have, all the men in suits. Now it's parted on the side, shaved down to show the white skin around his ears and at the back of his neck. The barber also shaved him; the skin of his face feels scraped raw, glowing with aftershave. His eyes water.

Inside, he stands at the window, waiting a while before a woman police officer appears on the other side.

"I'm here for Ray," he says.

"Pardon me?"

"I know he's in here. I figured it out."

"I'm sorry, I have no idea what you're talking about."

Scott lets his pack rest on the floor, unzips it. Unfolding the newspaper, he holds it up, the article facing her through the thick pane of glass.

"I'm his best friend," he says.

The officer's eyes swing away slowly, and then she looks at Scott again.

"Why don't you have a seat, sir? I'll see if I can find someone to speak with you."

"Appreciate it." He sits down in an orange plastic chair. The plastic is cracked and pinches his leg. He waits, and his mind leaps connections; he can't figure how he got to the thoughts he's thinking, and then he forgets them, and it starts over. He tries to concentrate on a poster, a colored drawing with phone numbers to call for every problem: fire, flood, abandoned vehicles, downed power lines, dead animals—

A door opens, and he's led through it, down a series of crooked hallways. Scott follows the officer. They stop at a door where the nameplate reads INSPECTOR LEWIS WATKINS. The officer knocks.

"It's open," a voice says.

"The gentleman we spoke about."

Scott knows enough to mistrust any situation where he's called a gentleman. He steps into the room.

"Inspector Watkins," he says. "I thought I'd better get down here, once I heard what was going on."

The Ambidextrist

The top of the inspector's head is shiny bald, and his eyebrows are thick, his cheeks hanging in slight jowls. He frowns, hesitating before shaking the hand Scott holds out. He gestures to a chair; a gold watch flashes on his thick wrist.

"It's been going on for three days, now," he says. "It took a little while for you to come forward."

"I've been away," Scott says. "Working."

"Someone do some work on your face?"

"That's all healing. It's old."

"And what is your line of work?"

"Medical, mostly. Health care, I guess you'd call it."

"I see. Did you tell me your name?"

"Scott."

"And now, Scott, this Mr. Ray is an acquaintance of yours?"

"A friend of mine. A close friend."

"How close?" the inspector says. "How exactly would you characterize your relationship?"

"I don't know what you're insinulating," Scott says. "He's a friend of mine."

"Please, sit down."

Scott's embarrassed to find he's still standing. He sits, trying to gather himself. Waves of heat prickle up his back, twist over his shoulders, tighten around his scalp. This is it, now, he's in the thick of it; he wills himself to be steady. Pieces of cut hair itch his neck. The walls are bare. There's one framed photograph on the desk, but it's turned away. The room has no windows, and it seems it might be underground, surrounded by layer after layer of rooms exactly like it, walls that cushion all sound.

"What are you smiling about?" the inspector says.

"Nothing, sir. I guess I was just trying to show my goodwill. By smiling, that is."

"Goodwill." He frowns again. "Very good."

Awake

Scott sees then that the inspector looks tired, as if he hasn't slept for days, either; this seems fair and right, since they're matching wits.

"Thing of it is, I know those boys don't like him," Scott says. "They were laying for him, you know. And you get boys together and they'll do anything, tell you anything to stay out of trouble."

"I'm well aware of that."

"I brought something," Scott says. Reaching down, he begins to unzip his pack.

"Easy there. Slow," the inspector says. "I'm armed."

"Inspector Watson," Scott says.

"Watkins."

"Inspector Watkins, I'm not stupid." Slowly, Scott withdraws his hand from the pack. The bills are in a thick stack, held together by rubber bands. Leaning forward, he sets them on the desk, then leans away again.

"Now what's this about?"

"Three thousand dollars," Scott says.

"I see that."

"Isn't that how it always works? That's bail."

The inspector picks up the money, thumbs the edges, and sets it down again, closer to him. Scott considers getting out the other eight hundred, but he doesn't want to spend it all unless he has no choice.

"I'm thinking," Inspector Watkins says, "that perhaps you don't have all the information that I have available to me."

"Exactly," Scott says. "That goes both ways."

"There's been a confession."

"No."

"That's what I said."

"I mean you can't really confess to an accident, or self-defense, which is what we're talking about here. Circumstances."

"How do you know all this? Were you there?" Inspector Watkins opens a drawer, drops the money into it, and locks it with a key.

189

"I told you, I've been away."

"Perhaps," the inspector says, "perhaps it wasn't your best friend Ray who confessed. Did you think of that?"

"But you didn't let him go."

"Perhaps we're holding him on suspicion of involvement in other cases."

"Listen," Scott says.

"Why don't you wait outside? We'll see what we can do." The inspector brings his hands together as if he and Scott have gotten somewhere, reached some agreement. "No promises, of course, and you'd have to vouch for him, give us an address where we can reach you, so we can find him."

Scott takes the pen and paper held out to him. Leaning over the desk, he writes the address of Ruth's house on Kater Street. It's the only address he knows.

Minutes later, he's escorted from the police station. He stands waiting, half under an awning so a line of shadow cuts straight up his body, bisecting his face. The right lens of his glasses has turned dark, while the other is still clear. He tries to decide if the sun or the shade might help him feel better.

Twenty-five

The Bridge

Ray does not ask any questions when they unlock his cell. The sergeant holds out his shoelaces, his belt, then leads him up the stairs, down a narrow hallway. He opens a door and pushes Ray out into the fresh air, the brightness.

Ray stumbles, hands up to shield his eyes. Bending down, fingers shaking, he threads the laces through, ties them; he slides his cracked belt through the loops of his pants. A shadow slides toward him, and when he looks up Scott is there, in a dark red shirt and crooked glasses.

"You knew it was me, didn't you? I been making money, or I'd have been here sooner."

Ray stands, lurching against Scott, steadying himself.

"Land legs," Scott says. "You'll be all right."

"You got yourself all pimped up," Ray says. "Haircut."

"Let's walk."

"That's right. Let's get away from here."

191

They head down the sidewalk, slowly, their shoulders almost touching. They walk a block and a half before Scott speaks.

"Haven't slept in four days."

"Not me," Ray says. "I've been dreaming. Sleeping all the time." He rakes at his hair, trying to work out the flat sections. The cramps in his legs come and go. "I could rest, though. Sleeping's not always the same as resting."

"Right on," Scott says. "Lead the way."

They reach the Franklin Parkway. The museum, lit by the sun, is only half a mile away.

"Which boy was it?" Scott says.

"I don't know. It doesn't matter."

"Black or white?"

"Black," Ray says. "Can we not talk about this right now?"

"Oh, yeah," Scott says. "Sorry. Man, we got all sorts of time. I'm a little wired, here, that's all."

They walk slowly, in silence, for ten minutes, and almost reach the river. They shuffle along Twenty-third Street, then over to Twenty-fourth. Finally, they turn underneath the shadow of the Walnut Street Bridge.

"Almost there," Ray says.

They pass a loading dock, then a pile of wet clothes, graffiti on the walls, some empty purses and wallets—all the little things people steal from cars, empty out, and leave behind. Closer to the river, the round concrete pillars rise, supporting the bridge. A ladder is bolted to the concrete, halfway up one pillar. Ray stacks two plastic milk crates, then balances on them, stretching for the ladder's bottom rung.

His arms tremble with the strain; he kicks with his feet until he's there, he's climbing. Ten more feet and he's at the bottom of the bridge, the underside; a dark, square opening leads into the space, only four feet high, just under the street. He steps off the ladder and crouches in the darkness, inside the thickness of the bridge.

Looking down, he sees Scott, squinting upward, climbing onto the milk crates.

"Kick those away," Ray hisses down, "so no one knows we're up here."

Scott gasps; his legs twist, and then he regains his grip. His face jerks closer and closer, until he's sitting next to Ray, breathing hard.

"What is this?" he says.

"It's famous in the winter," Ray says. "The steam pipes run through it—that keeps everyone warm."

There's no ventilation; the empty darkness smells like dirty clothes and sleeping bodies, though chances are there's no one here. Ray leads Scott deeper, now out above the river, hidden beneath their feet. The sharp claws of rodents scrabble nearby, invisible, on the asbestos-wrapped pipes. Ray leads him past the hammocks made of plastic mesh from construction sites, over piles of crushed aluminum cans. At last, his hands patting the air, he finds an old couch—pulled up here somehow, sometime—and it's narrow but there's room enough for the two of them to stretch out side by side.

"Thanks," Ray says. "I meant to say that. Whatever you did."

"That goes without saying."

"Sleep, now."

"All right," Scott says, his voice already trailing away. "I knew you were innocent."

Ray listens beyond Scott's breathing, until he is certain they are alone inside the bridge. Some nights in the winter, there's almost a hundred people, here—most of them messed up, one way or the other, and everyone getting into each other's business, trying to find out if you have anything they want. He avoids this place, even when the trees and bushes lose their leaves and cover is impossible to find. Now, though, it's the only place. He listens to the cars and buses, rattling overhead. All his chances are over, in this city. They'll run him down every time they can. Is he innocent? If anyone could understand his confession,

193

he'd give it to them. Because he's followed the boys, called to them, planned for them. He wanted the boys to come, expected it, willed it to happen. All but the last part, yet could he be responsible for everything but the ending, the result? He does not know. A boy is dead, and he sees how he set it all in motion.

Hours later, Scott awakens. Ray is sitting nearby in the darkness, still turning over the same thoughts.

"Ray?"

"I'm here."

"What time is it?"

"Does it matter? Sleep."

"If anything goes wrong, if we get split up, we'll meet in the garden," Scott says. "We have to stick together."

The bridge shakes with the traffic overhead. Ray coughs, sits back on the couch, leans against Scott's legs.

"I warned you about those boys, Ray."

"Yes, you did."

"Whatever it was," Scott says. "I could've helped you. You're the only one who ever really listened to me, at all."

"If I could have reached the garden," Ray says. "I could have put him on my bicycle, somehow."

"Whatever it was you wanted, I could do it."

"I wish," Ray says. "You're too old. That's all."

"And it won't take long before I get some more money together. We could get a car. Go anywhere. Just tell me what to do."

"Sleep," Ray says, reclining again. "I think I will, too."

Twenty-six

Forking Paths

G igantic faces smile down from the billboards. A hand holds a Tastykake as big as a house. The sun is still bright, yet weaker than a month ago. Men come out of the bushes and stare at John; he walks farther up the bank. He's been waiting along the river all morning.

Darnay comes through the fence, not the usual way. He wears gold earrings, tiny hoops, and his hair is cut in a low fade, perfectly flat on top. He doesn't reach out to shake John's hand.

"What up?"

"Nothing."

They both look at the ground, the dirty white gravel. John's got new basketball shoes; Darnay wears his same pair from last year, toes coming unstitched since his feet have grown.

"What are you doing there?" Darnay says. "What's going on with that?"

"Nothing." John had been scratching at his hip, not paying attention to what he was doing.

"Just itching your ass like that for no reason?" Darnay says. "Let's see your tattoo."

"Why?"

"Because I said so."

John tries to wait it out, but he has no choice. He pulls down the waistband of his shorts. The angled J is faded. Darnay leans closer, squints at the rows of tiny white lines crosshatched above the ink.

"They do it with lasers," John says. "A little at a time. Doesn't hurt."

"What happened to you?" Darnay says.

"My mom saw it."

"Why would she be looking at your naked ass?"

"She would've seen it, sometime."

"You told her," Darnay says. "Doesn't surprise me, but still."

"What am I supposed to do?"

"You want me to tell you?"

"I can't do anything."

"That's right," Darnay says.

Across the river, cars and trucks chase each other down the expressway. An inner tube, escaped from somewhere upriver, slips by, holding nothing as it slides beneath the bridge, bounces off a support, and is gone.

At Swan's funeral, John and Darnay had sat apart from each other. Terrell was there, too, the third point of a triangle. And Swan, lying there in a hand-me-down suit he never wore when he was alive. His coffin was too big, made for a man, so there was an extra foot of space up by his head. If his bones were broken, if he was bruised, all that had been hidden. His hands, folded together, resting across his stomach, looked like they might move. No one sang, and the church was half empty, all the bare pews behind them. Afterward, Swan's little sister, Zina, counted silently, her feet moving as if they were jumping rope.

Forking Paths

The funeral was the day after Swan died—there was no waiting; that was when their story was still holding, when everyone still blamed the old man. The boys denied that they'd even been at the waterworks that night, said they hadn't seen Swan since the morning before.

"Did Terrell tell?" John says.

"About us?" Darnay says. "If he did, we'd be where he is. Terrell won't tell. Someone like you—you'd tell in a second."

"I haven't."

"You will," Darnay says. "And it doesn't matter. But Terrell won't tell—I mean, he's still got his tattoo. You're the only one who doesn't, of all of us, now."

They're both silent for a moment; neither wants to think of the tattoo on Swan's body, inside that coffin, under the ground.

John looks up, tries to meet Darnay's eyes, but Darnay is looking past him, at something else.

Emerging from the bridge's shadow, into the sun, the man walks toward them, between the train tracks. He steps on every other tie with his cowboy boots, a stretch that makes him alternately grow and shrink as he approaches.

"He sees us," Darnay says.

Twenty-seven
The New Beginning

S cott awakens. Inside the bridge, it's impossible to say what time it is. "Ray?" he says.

There is no answer. Scott rolls from the couch, then crawls toward the pale glow, the hole where light seeps in. Carefully, slowly, he starts down the ladder. Hanging for a moment, he lands among the scattered milk crates. The balls of his feet burn. He steps on the leaning chain-link fence, forcing it all the way to the ground, and walks across it, onto the path that runs along the river. The gravel hurts his feet, so he walks between the train tracks, on the smooth wood of the ties.

Coming out of the darkness, into the light, it seems the brightness brings a new edge to every sense. His skin prickles under the weight of the sun; distant car engines, across the river on the expressway, roar. The billboards overhead are in full color and all promises, too hopeful to believe, holding everything he doesn't have. A pile of batteries shines between the tracks; he pockets a few, takes them as a sign that Ray is near.

He's less than twenty-five feet from the boys before he sees them, off to the left, next to the bushes. Only two of them, the white one and the biggest black one, and he doubts they'll dare to say anything. Not only are they silent, they pretend not to see him. As he walks past, he feels their eyes on him; he turns to face them.

"Where's your boy Terrell?" he says.

"Not here," the black one says.

"He alive?"

"Far as I know."

"Yes," the white one says.

"So what?" says the other, stepping forward, one fist raised.

Scott doesn't even bother to strike a jujitsu pose. Reaching into his pocket, he throws one battery, then the next; he throws them until they're gone, then starts with the biggest pieces of gravel he can find.

The boys back off until they're beyond his range. They stand there as if they might come after him, but he can tell by the way they move, checking each other, that there's not enough trust between them. When he takes a step forward, they take one back.

Scott stares them down, then turns away, continuing to walk upriver. At least, he thinks, it wasn't Terrell—that doesn't change the fact of what happened, but at least the dead boy is not Ruth's brother, is not someone Scott's talked to, whose name he knows.

Under the next bridge, the shadows are even darker. Scott almost trips over the bicycle before his eyes adjust and he recognizes it, right at the edge of the river, on a concrete slab. His skin tightens, cold around his bones. It's half taken apart, tires loose on the rims, spokes bent and broken, the makeshift rearview mirrors shattered. The plastic section of a car's grille that Ray had attached to the front is detached now, broken apart. The raccoon tail is torn in two.

He looks back for the boys—they're already gone, but they weren't behind this, they don't have it in them anymore. Turning back to the bicycle, he sees a pair of Ray's powder-blue dress pants, pulled inside out, twisted under the frame. It must have rained somewhere; the river is high, knuckling along, the color of caramel. It looks as if the old man jumped into the water—too much like that to believe it.

"This just isn't right," he says.

At his words, there's motion, off to the right. Two figures step closer, from deep in the shadows; he had not noticed them because they've been standing perfectly still.

"Damn good thing," Oliver says. "Here we were, waiting to have you explain to us what's right and what's wrong, Scotty." He's still wearing the same dirty tweed vest, the sandals, the stocking cap.

"What did you do with him?" Scott says.

"Who?"

"That's his bike."

"We just found it," the other man says. "In the bushes. Wasn't anyone attached to it."

"He didn't jump into the river," Scott says.

"What are you talking about?" Oliver says. It looks as if he's waxed his mustache; its tips point slightly upward. "Excuse my manners," he says. "Scott, this is my friend Steve-O. He's heard plenty about you."

Steve-O just nods. He wears a red flannel shirt with the arms torn off. His own arms are thick and doughy, ready to squeeze the life out of something. The curls on his head are so blond they're almost white. In one fist, he holds an adjustable wrench; in the other, a screwdriver. Bending down, he sharpens the screwdriver—one side, then the other—on the concrete.

"You still look tired," Oliver says. "Like regular hell."

"Appreciate it," Scott says.

"He always was a big talker," Oliver says to Steve-O, "but here lately Scotty's been humbled some."

Hidden cars shake the bridge overhead, then appear, blurs of color, as they merge onto 676. Scott thinks of his eight hundred dollars, still in his backpack, as far as he knows.

"Wouldn't mind seeing you tangle with Steve-O," Oliver says. "He'd do it, tear a piece out of you, if I said the word. Isn't that right?"

"Yep," Steve-O says.

"I have to go," Scott says. "Maybe another time. Later."

"Later means never," Oliver says.

"Things to do," Scott says. He heads into the sunlight, not looking back. Behind him, he hears Oliver's voice.

"Busy, busy, busy."

Scott avoids the waterworks; he knows it's wrapped in yellow police tape, and he doesn't like the sight. Climbing the rise and crossing the grass park, then Vine Street, he picks up speed. People run up and down the steps of the museum, exercising, taking pictures of each other. He doesn't know what day it is anymore—if it was a free Sunday, if he had the time, he'd go inside, sit down on a bench and let it all loose inside him. But he has no time. He shuffles along Kelly Drive, then crosses it.

A pigeon's been hit and run over, smashed dead, flat except for one wing, which flaps up and down with the wind of passing cars. Tin cans riddle the bushes on the other side. Condoms. Scott's through the bushes, branches scratching his bare arms. He comes out onto more blacktop, past an abandoned car, burned out, resting on its chassis; he skirts a baseball diamond, empty except for an old man hitting a golf ball ten feet at a time and a woman with a dog bigger than she is, letting it run.

The dog doesn't notice Scott as he slips into the woods again, under the trees. Squirrels leap from branch to branch, talking the whole time. His energy comes in hot surges, lapses into exhaustion, then fires up again. Mansions flash through the leaves and branches—the colors of paint, straight slants of rooftops—and then they're gone again. He can hear the cars below, down on Kelly Drive, but he can no longer see them. He wishes someone would call his name. His legs keep going, moving him through it all. Leaves slither around him.

Vines tangle his ankles, can't hold him back. Spiderwebs wrap his face, across his glasses, and he hardly notices.

The entrance is hidden, but he knows the way; the tiny bells hang from the fishing line, strung through the bushes, and he doesn't try to cup the bells in his hands, to muffle their ringing.

He steps into the clearing and stands there, amazed, taking it all in.

Wooden animals are scattered about, some stamped straight into the mud, only their heads above the surface; some of the spoons are bent double, their photographic faces hidden, while others are so faded their features are lost. Footprints mark the dirt—painted stones, shards of mirrors and glass shine from the beneath the bushes, where they have been kicked. Chicken bones are scattered, splintered. In the pool, the plastic lining has torn, and all the water is gone; already, the bright green shoots of new plants fill the rounded indentation.

The sun, straight overhead, makes Scott shiver. Bending, he gently touches the new sprouts in the pond. He picks up a row of keys, pockets them. The main thing is that he saw the garden before this, that he won't forget, that he knew the man who made it beautiful. He was right to bail Ray out—it was a responsibility that couldn't be sidestepped. And he wasn't mistaken about Ray, but that doesn't mean the old man had to stay. It's like with Chrissie—if someone gets in that far and burns him, he knows, that doesn't mean his own feelings weren't real; those muscles worked, and are stronger, ready to hold better the next time.

Next to Scott's foot, a rusted scissors rests, one blade stuck in the mud; he pulls it out, seeing white hairs along the other blade's edge. And then, under a bush, he notices something else. A whole line of white hairs, clumps of black ones, all blown to collect along a stick on the ground. Stepping closer, he rakes the hairs together with his fingers. Bristly, some whiskers, some longer. He spreads them more sparsely, more widely, as he walks from the garden, between the bushes, and under the trees.

Twenty-eight

☰ Letter

There are boys here who enjoy beating on another person. Terrell understands that, since he's felt the same way. Some mornings he spits up blood; some of his ribs feel splintered, sharp.

It can come at night, or with any lapse in supervision. Quick and savage, since the boys never know how long they have. They try to bruise the face less—that shows. And if he lets anyone see the bruises under his clothes, that's as bad as snitching. All he can do is protect his balls, and then, once he goes down, curl up and let them work on his back.

He had not told on Darnay or John, he has not, though maybe they believe he has—the boys here believe they know something; they call him snitch, squealer, worse. While they beat him, they repeat their names, daring him to tell.

They ask him if he's afraid, and he always says he is. There isn't a right answer to that question. His ribs are bruised, his hips, the long bones of his thighs. He never fights back, and that makes the boys more angry. They want to provoke him, to bring him down to where they are; in the midst of it, he doesn't so much feel pain as relief that the waiting is over, even if it's about to start again. And he feels he deserves every punch, every kick.

The sun seems higher in the sky here, farther away. He wears a stiff shirt, the pants that are not his own, the whole outfit worn by someone else before him; a whole line stretches back, other boys handing down their missteps and mistakes, some ashamed and some not. His black leather boots are the same as everyone's—no laces, a zipper up the side, two sizes too big.

Today he walks circles, around and around a field of dirt. There are fences on every side; low, but there's no reason to climb them, nowhere to go. Fields stretch beyond on every side, with hardly a hill, all the trees far away. Crows sit atop the fence, unevenly spaced. Once, Terrell walked all the way to the edge, and the crows just cawed at him. They didn't even unfold their black wings.

The sun is so weak he can stare into it. The day is hot, though, sticky. He sweats, then shivers. Looking up, he sees a plane flying over, slicing through the clouds.

The hour is almost up. Some of the other boys are over on the blacktop, playing basketball. The game is only an excuse to get on the wrong side of someone, to do or say something you'll pay for later, and if a fight starts on the court, the counselors will just watch it for a while—for their entertainment, and to let the boys wear themselves out. There are some big kids in here, much bigger, much meaner than Darnay. Country boys, Spanish-speaking boys, some from Philadel-phia, not far from Terrell's own neighborhood. There are others who are preyed upon, too; they cluster together, trying for safety in num-bers, flinching when someone reaches for the salt. Terrell doesn't need that kind of friend. After a week, he already draws less attention; more recent arrivals are more interesting—new boys with new weaknesses to explore.

He steps on his faint shadow as he turns a corner. The shadow slides around him, taking another angle. He misses Ruth holding him, his big sister sleeping heavy beside him, and he misses Swan. Not because Swan is dead, but because he'd feel better if Swan were here. And not so much to talk to, just to stand beside him, to walk these circles.

He feels half asleep, time blowing around him. Here there is no comfort like Swan or Ruth, here there is only the row of bunk beds and the hope that he will not be the first one to fall asleep. Boys whisper, asking if he's awake, and it is a mistake not to answer. He's made that mistake before.

If he felt comfortable, that might mean he belongs, which he does and he doesn't. He can see how his time will pass. He can see that it will. The nighttime, then breakfast, exercise, lunch, time inside with the books and the ten-year-old video games, and then the counseling sessions, and dinner, into the showers, and then the bunks again.

The other boys had laughed at his tattoo in the shower, but they still wanted to know how he got it, if it meant anything more than the first letter of his name. Swan had given it to him, put the ink under his skin; he would not, could not forget that. If he started, he'd tell everything, and the boys did not deserve to know about Swan.

That night at the waterworks, Terrell was laughing wild, the moon above, the machine lurching under him; the headlights swept jerkily back and forth, catching Swan's shoes, then the top of his head. And then the stars buckled and slid away. Terrell bit his tongue, lost his grip. The ground reared up.

Darnay scrambled over the top of him and Terrell followed; there was nothing to push off against and then the ground came chopping beneath his feet, the air crashing around him.

Then he was outside the fence, the buildings inside, and he

couldn't remember sliding under, couldn't remember climbing over. His wrists ached from how he landed, on all fours and already moving, arms and legs going in midair, eager to touch anything.

They gathered, the three of them, shouting, drawn together, and then moved backward, through the bushes, against the cliff. They called Swan's name, but he did not answer; John still had hold of his walkie-talkie, and they tried that, too. Nothing but static.

"He's probably halfway home by now," Darnay said, and then they heard the sirens—still distant, but definitely on the way.

First, it was only one police car. An officer got out, then climbed back in, and the car eased into the gate until the chain snapped. And then a whole string of vehicles, all the sirens going, all swerving to a stop, men waving to hold back, to not get too close. The red lights flashed along the white walls of the buildings, spun in and out of the pillars.

Men approached the dark edge of the hole, slowly, their hands out in front like the ground might give way and suck them down. None of it made sense. They shouted down into the hole, words that couldn't be understood. Some of the men had their pistols out, pointing down. The hole swallowed all the spotlights' brightness.

And then the old man came out of the building behind all the policemen, carrying something over his shoulder. No one noticed until he was close, and then they turned, all together, guns drawn.

When they took Swan away from him, the old man fought, and when they led him away he was trying to get back, trying to see what was happening. The paramedics surrounded Swan. The policemen got the old man's hands behind his back, pushed his head down, forced him into one of their cars.

They turned the spotlights to shine into the bushes, and the boys flattened out on their stomachs, breathing dirt, not moving at all. What else were they supposed to do?

Swan was strapped onto a stretcher, rushed away in the ambulance, and the boys sat still, not moving or talking until all the cars and trucks and lights were gone. Then, one by one, they stood and walked to the fence. On the other side, halfway to the dark, ragged edges of the hole, were Swan's shoes, left behind, and pieces of his clothing, where they'd been torn and cut and thrown aside.

The moon dimmed and slid behind clouds; the headlights across the river became scarcer and scarcer. Then, Terrell out in front, the boys walked away, under the overpass, past people sleeping, past whispers in the bushes. They climbed into an empty boxcar and sat there, unwinding a series of possible stories. Low voices echoing, faces hidden in the darkness, they wanted to handle the night, to make sense of it while they still could. None of the stories they expected to use—they would wait to see what happened to Swan, see what he said—but when things turned out the way they did, it was the story with the old man in the middle that worked out best.

That story would have held, most likely, except Terrell had a harder and harder time repeating it, knowing how the blame was coming to rest, wondering what Swan would think. So Terrell told, at least his part, and that is how he ended up here.

Here where they always want to talk with him. It was only trespassing, destruction of property—unless, they said, he still had more to tell them. He'll be out after school has already started, but they say he can probably catch up, probably won't lose a year. All he knows is when he returns to the city things will have changed. He can't return to where he was—that place no longer exists.

Often, Terrell thinks of Lakeesha. She had not been at Swan's funeral; he expected her there, maybe only because he was afraid to see her. He has written Lakeesha letters, but he has not sent them. Writing to her is almost like explaining himself to Swan, trying to. He admits what he did, owns up to the lies he's told. He tells her he didn't lie because of what he saw her do with Swan in the woods, and then admits maybe it was, that that's part of what he was after—only it was her way of talking, too, joking about clotheslines and dogs and her eyes on his, daring him. Maybe it's too late to be honest, but still he wants to say it, what kind of friend he's been, the way he feels now. In his letters, he asks her to send him her necklace, tells her he wants to loose the teeth from their string, spill them rattling across a tabletop; that he wants to line them up, their sharp edges in his hand; that he wants to put one in his mouth and think of her.

Would she even open a letter from him? If he knocked on her door, would she unlock it?

The horn is blowing now, and the counselors echo it with their whistles. Terrell has five minutes to be inside the building. He begins walking back across the field.

Twenty-nine

≡ Keys

No one can stop a thing like that from happening—this is what people tell Ruth. She is not certain she believes it, yet she tries to tell herself that this was a lucky turn, that Terrell will get out and never go back in, never fall through the ground or anything like it. She tells herself that it's a kind of relief that he found some actual trouble and is still alive—that the fact of it is easier than the waiting.

Still, at first she could not make herself believe any of this. Hysterical, she tried to climb the walls inside her house, tore plaster loose; she drew all over her face with ballpoint pens, all up and down her arms. She wandered through the rooms of her house, eyes open but not seeing, bouncing off walls, caught in corners, and she walked the streets of the neighborhood, late at night, and along the banks of the river. Once, the police picked her up—telling her not to look for trouble where it wasn't hard to find—and, always, Dwayne watched her. He let her go, but kept her from hurting herself. He said she had to get it out, so it wouldn't show on the days she visited Terrell. If she'd failed her little brother, it wasn't all the way. Not yet.

Now, in the screen, a purse slides past, with a smaller one inside it—the dark circles of coins, lipsticks like bullets, the edges shadowy. Ruth looks up just in time to see him coming. Scott. In a red shirt and new slacks, waving as he approaches.

She looks back to the scanner just in time to stop a baby from going through, its carrier pulled along the conveyor belt. The baby's mother gives Ruth an accusatory look, then moves on, through the metal detector. When Ruth glances up again, Scott is closer. A ring of keys jangles at his waist, attached to a belt loop. He carries his blue jacket under one arm, and he's smiling too widely; the people around him look nervous.

"Ruth," he says. "You been worried about me?"

"Not exactly," she says.

She waits for him to keep moving, toward whatever it is that he does when he comes here, but he steps to the side, then stands next to her, close enough to touch. His hair is shorter and wet. She can see the trail of a comb's teeth, smooth lines all around his head. It smells like he's wearing some kind of cologne, or has washed with scented soap.

"I got to talk with you," he says.

"I'm working." Ruth watches the screen, speaks without taking her eyes from it.

"This is a serious thing," Scott says.

"Listen—" She turns toward him, and her braids swing out, beads rattling against the screen.

"Ruth," José calls from the other security station. "There a problem over there?"

"Yes," she says. "No. Not really. Could you watch this side for a second?"

She steps away, Scott staying close. They stand together, silent, people milling past them.

"Well?" she says.

"That was a good thing Terrell did," he says.

"He told the truth. What else would he do?"

"Well, he saved a friend of mine a lot of trouble. That's beyond certain."

"Don't start saying you warned me," Ruth says.

"It's something else," he says. "You're not going to like it, so I'm just going to try to say it straight."

"Right now," she says, "I don't have a lot of patience."

"I was wrong—well, I'm not sure how to say this."

"That's a decent start."

"I mean," he says, "things between us, they're not going to work out like the way it seemed everything was heading, you know. I hoped it would, but now I lost it somehow. I can't."

Ruth just listens. Over Scott's shoulder, a man pushes a floor buffer, its round head smoothly circling. The way she feels, listening, surprises her. It is closer to sympathy or tenderness than it is to anger, and she isn't certain how to react. Finally, she nods, agreeing with him.

"Ruth!" José calls. "Hand check."

"Thank you," she says to Scott, and steps away, around him.

She watches as he hunches his shoulders, slips his arms through the straps of his pack, and sets it down. It's pulled into the scanner and disappears through the rubber tendrils. When he steps forward, the keys at his waist set off the metal detector. He holds out his arms, and she waves the wand all around him.

"You're fine," she says.

"All right, then," he says, touching her shoulder.

He walks down the terminal, people surrounding him. Some run past, weaving through the oncoming traffic; others walk slowly, holding hands, reunited and going home. Men drive carts full of old people, beep high-pitched horns. Scott steps aside, then keeps walking. He believes Ruth still watches him, but he does not look back to check. He doesn't want to be mistaken.

211

The Ambidextrist

Sitting in the waiting area of gate E7, he stares at people until they feel his gaze and look up; then he looks away. Men and women check their watches, open briefcases on their laps, try to control their children. When his row is called over the loudspeaker, he stands, hands over his boarding pass, then steps through the door, down the slanted floor of the jetway, past the black accordion of rubber that attaches it to the plane. He steps on board.

He finds his seat and sets his pack on the floor by his feet, where he can keep an eye on it. The window next to him is plastic, double paned, lined with scratches. Unlatching the tray table, he unfolds it, then folds it up again. He feels the hardened chewing gum in the arm-rest ashtray, stuck there, and reads the plastic card with red arrows, pointing to the emergency exits. When he turns to find the exit nearest him, he sees other people twisting the nozzles above their heads; he does the same, and it spits lukewarm air down into his face. He twists it back off before it messes up his hair.

Somewhere behind him, a baby is crying.

"Jesus," a voice says. "They shouldn't fly, that young."

The plane begins to move, slowly backing out; the nose swings around and they're heading toward the runway. For luck, Scott holds the keys on the ring at his waist; they are from the garden and open nothing, but they're valuable reminders.

Suddenly, the plane begins to accelerate. The grooves in the concrete click by faster and faster, the tall grass along the runway a blur, the world sliding past. And then his seat tilts back and the ground angles away—the plane is detached from it, climbing.

They rise into a cloud, where there is nothing but terrifying white, where there's no way anyone could tell where they're going, or how many other planes or flocks of geese or hot air balloons are also inside the whiteness, and then they pass through, out the top, leveling off. The sky is a dark, dark blue. For a moment it feels like they're under water—a color like this must be thicker than air. It slows the plane.

212

Keys

The ground hardly moves down below. The clouds thin and scatter; their shadows settle darkly through the city as the plane's shadow, pointed south, slides away from it all. Scott is headed toward a place he's never been, and that makes him feel hopeful and afraid. He watches the tall buildings, the green expanse of the park, all the places he's walked and slept; he sees the black grid of streets where cars wait for each other and crawl along, the white stone of the museum. The Schuylkill's dark water twists slowly through the land.

Perhaps Ray is down below, running, avoiding towns and houses, beneath the cover of trees, arms and legs scratched by branches as he stumbles and stays on his feet, as he drives birds and animals out ahead of him. Bald, he spits bugs from his teeth, not stopping, searching for something—perhaps even for Scott—and always checking behind him, never certain what he'll be blamed for, now, and knowing how hard it is to explain when situations tangle. People catch sight of Ray, a shape in the trees, but then they lose track and become uncertain what they saw.

Or perhaps he's walking through another city. Clean-shaven, in a new suit. Greeting people on the street, generous with his cigarettes and all that advice. He's reading a newspaper with friends around him, or looking through a window at a line of bicycles.

The plane leaves the city, then the suburbs behind. The country-side opens up, as if gravity is heavier and holds down some places; then it relents and goes slack to allow hills and mountains to rise. Scott watches, his thoughts slow and straying. He's still not sleeping well, and part of that is how much he misses Ray. Chances are he'll never again be held by, feel those arms around him.

213

≡ Acknowledgments

All gratitude to the Vinings and the Rocks. To Ira Silverberg: unbeliev-able. To Beau Friedlander, for belief. Vast insight and generosity are possessed by Greg Changnon, Susan Choi, Stacey D'Erasmo, Steve Lattimore, Nancy Packer, and Roy Parvin. Thanks to the National Endowment for the Arts. And, for being fairly careful with my body, to the doctors and technicians at SmithKline Beecham and in the neu-ropsychiatric trials at the University of Pennsylvania. Finally, a debt to Adnan "Blade" Husain, Pat Parelli, and all other Natural Horse-Men.